TEXAS COWBOY

WISHBONE TEXAS #1

ANN B. HARRISON

Texas Cowboy
Wishbone Texas #1
Copyright © 2020 Ann B. Harrison

CHAPTER ONE

Duke Wilson put the cash in the safe, shut the door and spun the dial with a sigh of relief. Thank the Lord this night was finally over. He rolled his shoulders, stood up and stretched his back. Too long bending over his desk doing the books after a full day on his feet was giving his body aches he didn't want to acknowledge. It made him feel older than his thirty-four years. Technically still a young buck. Shame his body didn't get the message.

He flicked off the light, stepped out of his office and shut the door behind him with a resounding thud. Three years of hard slog and finally he was beginning to see the steady income and repeat customers. You didn't start a business like a restaurant and hope for quiet evenings trade.

"Night, Duke." His kitchen hand walked toward him, dark shadows under his eyes.

He patted him on the back as he passed. "Night, Chris. Thanks for a great night's work. I'll see you tomorrow." He followed the young man down the hallway toward the back entrance to let him out. "Get some rest, you hear? It's going to be a big one. We have a few large parties coming in. Maybe after the weekend it will slow down and we can all catch up."

"I will. About time you headed home too. You've been here since before lunch yesterday." Chris pulled on his jacket before he got to the back door of the restaurant.

"Don't you worry about me. I'll look at hiring a new manager tomorrow."

"So you still haven't heard from the woman who was s'posed to start today?"

"Nope." Duke tried to keep the venom from his voice as he opened the back door and saw the young man out before locking it behind him. All he needed to do was a quick round of the restaurant to make sure everything was ready for the lunch crowd tomorrow, check the kitchen and double check the gas was off, and the windows and doors locked, and then he could head for home.

Duke covered all bases in record time before grabbing his keys. He went to the back door, opened it and armed the alarm before pulling it shut behind him. He skipped down the stairs to the parking lot and pulled up short. A dark SUV was parked near his truck. *What the heck?* He slowed his pace. His muscles tensed, on edge, alert as he approached, each step a whisper on the ground.

If someone was waiting to rob him, they would be shit out of luck. He made it a policy to never carry the days takings. Everything was locked away in the safe for pick up the following day by armored guards. He slid his keys in his back pocket to leave his hands free and approached the darkened vehicle.

A sudden movement in the driver's seat made him jump back. A woman's sleepy face appeared at the window. Her eyes locked onto his. She screamed.

Holy crap!

Duke held up his hands, trying to calm her down before things got out of control. She sucked in a breath, her hand on her chest. He indicated that she should open her window and after giving him a wary glance, she let it down a couple of inches, still keeping a wary look on her face.

"Yes?"

He crouched to try and minimize her fear, mindful of the tremor in her voice. Last thing he wanted to do was frighten her more than she already was.. "What're you doing here? I'm about to close up the parking lot. You should move on."

Defiance flared in her eyes. "Lock it up? You can't do that."

"Look, lady. I can do what I like. I own the place and I lock it up at night. Now if you don't want your vehicle stuck in here until lunchtime tomorrow when I get back, I suggest you go park it somewhere else."

"Duke Wilson?"

He stared at her hard trying to place the face or the voice. "And you would be?"

A bundle in the back seat moved and he heard the voice of a young boy through the crack in the window. "Mom. I'm cold."

His stomach dropped. What next? "You have a child in there? Listen, lady, do you need help?"

She wound the window all the way down, a look of resignation on her tired face. She patted a hand to her hair and looked down at her lap before she spoke. "I'm Cora Hamilton. Your new restaurant manager."

Crap. This wasn't how he wanted to greet his new employee. He wanted to see her over his office desk and tear her out for not showing up when she'd said she would. Preferably yesterday when she'd promised to arrive and take up her position.

Her chin rose a fraction. "Sorry I didn't make it yesterday. We had car problems and couldn't get here any earlier." She bit her lip and looked down at her hands again.

"You should've called. I was about to hire someone else or squash the position."

"Mom."

"I'm sorry. It was unavoidable. Everything went wrong. I called when I left but nobody answered – the restaurant must have been shut. And we were on the road early this morning and I thought it better to get here as soon as I could rather than keep trying to call." She turned around and spoke to the child in the back seat. "Lay down and try to sleep."

Duke could hear his mother's voice in his ear chiding him to mind his manners and help where he could, especially those less fortunate than himself. "Why are you sleeping in the car? Surely you'd arranged for somewhere to go before you moved to Wishbone."

"We did but since we're running late, they let the apartment to someone else and didn't bother to let me know until I arrived. All the motels I tried were full so we had no choice. I was planning on looking for something after I started work. Even if I have to look as far afield as Waco, I'll do it."

The town of Waco might look close on the map but it was a good thirty-five minutes away in light traffic. Not ideal for someone who would be keeping long hours. "You should've called me."

"I tried, okay?" Fire burned in her eyes before the shutters came down and her expression turned neutral.

"You can't stay here."

Her throat moved as she swallowed. Cora glanced away, and he couldn't see her reaction.

"I…"

"See that black truck? It's mine. Follow me home. You can have the guest room for the night." Duke cut her off before she could protest, hoping she wasn't getting the wrong idea.

Her head whipped around, eyes wide, staring at him, her mouth open.

Duke held up his hands ready to calm her down before she got the wrong message. "Don't worry. I live on the family ranch. My mom would kill me if she found out I'd left you here when there're perfectly good bedrooms at home you could use." He felt silly blaming his mother but it was true. She'd string him up if she found out this woman and her child were sleeping rough. Grandpa would take great pleasure in helping her too. Especially if it was for a staff member and most definitely a woman and child. Duke'd never live it down. Besides, nobody argued with his mama. Not if they knew what was good for them.

"I can't. I don't even know you."

"You came clear across Texas to work for me, so I guess that gives you some cred."

A quick smile flitted across her lips. "You came highly recommended and I needed a job."

"So did you. I don't normally employ someone without a personal interview so I guess that makes us even. Bo Reid recommended you as someone who was perfect for the job and I guess he said enough nice things about me too for you to make the trip without meeting face to face." He'd been livid before, but it sounded like she really had experienced a bit of a rough trot. Surely she deserved a second chance. "Now I meant what I said. You can't stay here. I won't hear of it. Besides, I think that little guy could use a decent bed by the look of it." He pointed his key fob and clicked his truck unlocked. "Follow me. It's not that far—about fifteen minutes out of town."

~

Cora turned on the engine.

"Mom, are we going with the man?"

"I guess so." He was her new boss, after all and probably kinder than she deserved after letting him down. And he came with high recommendations from Bo. He'd been a great employer but when she made the decision to leave, Bo hadn't been able to praise Duke Wilson enough. Insisted she'd be thankful she made the move and took the job on offer, not that he wanted to lose her but her safety was more important. She was good at her job. She trusted Bo. He'd been a great boss and friend but when she had decided to head clear across the state, he'd urged her to head to the small town of Wishbone just out of Waco.

"Duke will make sure you and Toby are looked after. I'd trust the guy with my own mother."

"Do your seat belt up sweetheart. Let's go find us a nice warm bed." She followed the black truck out of the parking lot and waited while Duke shut and locked the gates, then tailed him out of town. It didn't seem long before he pulled off the main road, drove for a little bit longer into the country and pulled up at a set of big white gates, stone posts either side. Perched across the top was a big wrought iron sign with the words, 'Lakeside Ranch' and a set of Texas longhorn horns either side.

"Are we there, Mom?"

"Sure looks like it."

Toby yawned. "Good. I'm really tired."

It'd been a long trip made even longer because her vehicles radiator sprung a leak before she got to the halfway point. She'd had to fork out money she hadn't counted on spending to repair it and pay for the motel they'd stayed in the night before last. Money she'd put aside for rent. Not that she needed it after losing the apartment but sooner or later, she'd have to find somewhere to stay.

Cora followed the tail lights down the long driveway, passing under massive oak trees either side until they came to a mansion. There were no other words to describe the huge home she pulled up at. Two story with an attic, wide wrap around verandas and manicured gardens were a far cry from the last motel she stayed at. This was like something out of a Dallas television episode and in the light of day, she knew it would be even more incredible than it looked under lights.

Duke got out of his truck and came to her door. Cora opened it, still a little wary. Most people weren't that…nice. Or charismatic, come to think of it. She shook her head as if waking from sleep. There was no place for thoughts like that. She had a child to raise and protect. Nothing else mattered.

"This is it. Home. What can I carry for you?"

"Nothing." She scrambled for her overnight bag and slid out before opening the back door. "I'm fine, thank you. Toby, grab your backpack and let's go. We don't want to disturb these kind people any more than we have to." It was hard to keep the tiredness and frustration from her voice, especially when Duke was helping her.

Duke held the door. "Don't worry about that. Not much will wake these guys. You can have my brother Clay's room. He lives in town now." He took her overnight bag from her hand despite her protest and skipped up the front steps. He turned and waited while she helped Toby. "He's the sheriff in case you wanted another referral of our family credentials."

When she reached the porch, he moved to open the front door. "Do you want anything to eat before you go up? A cup of coffee?"

Cora shook her head, despite the rumbling in her belly and the yearn for a good hot cup of caffeine. "Thanks but we're fine."

"Follow me." He walked in, held the door for them as Cora stood awestruck looking at the inside of the house. The entranceway alone was bigger than her last apartment.

An antique coat rack with a padded chair was tucked to one side, a range of Stetson's hanging on the pegs along the top. Some used and weathered with age, some looked brand new. A coat hung on one hook and an antique looking leather saddlebag hung next to it. Plump cushions, one with a map of Texas and the other handstitched with bluebonnets, were propped on the back of the seat. Whoever did the decorating had an eye for detail. It looked like it was straight out of a home magazine shoot.

To the right, low lamps shone over a large family living room. Heavy leather furniture cried out to be sat on. The wrinkles of age and wear only added to the inviting feeling of the room that looked as inviting and perfect as the entrance way.

He moved past her and indicated the staircase. "This way, folks."

Cora grabbed Toby's hand and helped him up the stairs. Their footsteps were deadened by the thick carpet tread running up the middle of the polished wooden boards. Intricate black iron held a wooden rail that Duke ran his hands over as he climbed.

At the top of the stairs, he turned left and Cora followed. Two doors down, he paused. "This here is your room." He opened the door and flicked on a light switch. A huge bed sat in the middle of the room, decked out with a padded comforter topped off with inviting pillows, and her body sung its praises. One night in a cheap motel and another in the front seat of her truck hadn't done her any favors.

"Wow." Toby let go of her hand and ran inside. He dumped his bag on the floor and clambered up on the bed to snuggle down.

"Toby, shoes off, buddy." The last thing she wanted was dirty shoe marks on the warm moss green cover. She felt enough guilt already just by being here.

"Don't fuss. This house is made for living in. Mama would have a fit if you treated it any other way." He moved inside and placed her bag next to the tallboy, indicating another door to the left of the bed. "Bathroom is through there. My room is next door so if you need anything, holler." He smiled. "Welcome to Wishbone, Cora. We'll discuss the job tomorrow, or later today if you want to be precise." He moved over to the door. "Sleep in. I don't surface until about nine or so. But if you want food or coffee, head downstairs to the left of where we came in past the staircase. You'll find the kitchen easy enough just by following your nose. Night now." He closed the door and left her standing there taking with him the small bubble of anticipation that'd crept into her space.

Her shoulders slumped with exhaustion mixed with a hefty dose of relief. Spending the night in the parking lot wasn't how she wanted to remember her arrival.

Toby stared at her from under droopy eyelashes.

"Come on, buddy. Teeth and then you can snuggle down and we can both get some much needed sleep." She held her hand out to him. "Tomorrow we can go exploring, but not until I wake up, okay?"

Toby nodded and as Cora's head hit the pillow, it was to the soundtrack of soft snores from the one man she could trust in the world.

. . .

C ora woke with a start. Something didn't feel right. She opened her eyes, and took a moment to get her bearings. Sunlight streamed through the window, dancing golden beams across the bedspread and over the dark timber furniture. The bed was so comfortable she could imagine being in a five star hotel and she didn't want to move and break the image in her mind.

She reached out a hand and patted the pillow beside her. Crap! Toby wasn't cuddled up next to her. She scrambled out of bed, used the bathroom and pulled on some wrinkled clothes from her bag. The last thing she'd said to him as they snuggled up in that ridiculously comfy bed was to stay in the room until she was awake. Why did her son have to be such an inquisitive child?

She flattened her hair into some sort of neatness by raking her fingers through it and opened the door. She peeked left and right and didn't see anyone or hear any movement. Cora walked over to the stairs and made her way down to the foyer feeling like an intruder. The living room was empty, and she followed Duke's directions to let her nose guide her toward the back of the house, taking the passageway to the rear of the stairs. As she got closer to the tantalizing smell, she could hear Toby giggling.

Sunlight filled the back facing kitchen and Cora paused at the door. If she thought the living room was big and inviting, this room blew her mind. It was a massive space that would do any restaurant proud. A large marble island was pride of place surrounded by about eight stools running down one side. Her son, looking like he belonged, was perched on one of those cowhide stools. He turned his head, his eyes met hers, and he broke out into a huge grin, the dimples in his freckled cheeks deepening. "Mama!

"Toby. I told you to stay with me." She walked in, smiled at the woman standing at the bench across from him, ready to make her apologies. "Good morning. I'm sorry about invading your home like this."

"You're Cora. Welcome to Lakeside Ranch. I hope you slept well, sugar."

Her welcoming smile was infectious and Cora smiled back, and stepped toward her. "Thank you so much for letting me stay. Not that I'd planned on it, mind. Duke was kind enough to offer, but I didn't mean to put anyone out and I did tell Toby to stay in the room until I woke up but he didn't and…" She stopped, aware that she was blathering on and probably making a fool of herself.

"Stop." The friendly woman held up her hand, a big smile spreading across her face all the way to her dark brown eyes. "You don't have to say a thing. I'm Duke's mom, Barbara. Everyone calls me Babs. Have a seat and I'll pour you a coffee. Toby was just telling me how he likes his eggs."

"Oh, you don't have to…

The smile flashed across her face again. "Cora. I like to feed people. It's what I do. Now stop fussing, sugar and let me have my fun." Babs took a pot off the stove and filled a large mug before she passed it over the counter top to Cora, who settled on one of the stools beside her son. "Cream and sugar?"

"No, thanks. This is fine." She wrapped her hands around the mug and lifted it to her lips, desperate for a soothing sip. She wasn't used to going without her fix me up for so long.

"So, you're going to be working for Duke. I'm pleased to hear it. That poor boy is run off his feet trying to do everything for himself." She grabbed her wooden spoon and stirred whatever was in the pan.

"Mama, stop exaggerating." Duke walked in, looking better than sin. Worn denim jeans rode low on his hips, a checked shirt that he hadn't buttoned up exposed just a hint of sun-kissed skin and his hair was damp from the shower. He padded over to his mom, bare feet slapping on the slate floors, kissed her on the forehead and gave her a hug before he grabbed his own cup of coffee.

"You work too hard. Been telling you that for years." She pushed him toward the island and grabbed another skillet, putting it on the massive gas cooker. "About time you took on someone to do the management side of things. Might see more of your gorgeous face now Cora is here." She patted his cheek to give her words more meaning and Cora almost melted at the action.

Duke grinned, moved to the island and perched up beside her. He grabbed the cream jug and poured a steady stream into his mug, then spooned in a heap of sugar granules and stirred it before he spoke. "How did you sleep?"

His husky voice rolled over her shoulders and sent a shiver down her spine. "Fantastic. Thank you." She held her hands around her mug. "It's really good of you to let me stay. I appreciate it."

"Anyone is welcome here, Cora, so don't go thinking you're putting us out. Too many empty rooms in this house far as I'm concerned." Babs pulled a tray of bacon out of the refrigerator and started to lay the slices in the hot pan. The fat sizzled and Cora's mouth watered. It took all of her willpower not to rub her belly in anticipation.

"Mama lives to smother people in her brand of love, don't you Mama?" He winked at Cora.

"Way I was raised, sugar. Ain't nothing wrong with being kind and helping out a stranger either."

"It was very kind of you regardless. I appreciated the bed." Cora sniffed the bacon cooking and her belly rumbled letting everyone know how hungry she was. She quickly pressed her hand against it, ignoring the snigger from Toby.

Babs scooped scrambled eggs from another pan onto a plate, added two slices of buttered toast and put it in front of Toby. His eyes bugged and a huge smile lit up his face.

Cora nudged him.

"Thank you, ma'am."

"You're welcome, Toby. Eat up now and then you can go down to the barn with Grandpa and see the animals. I bet he could use a strong little guy like you to give him a hand today."

Her son grinned but Cora reacted before he could get too excited. "Oh no, he doesn't need to do that. We have to go into town and find another apartment and check in with the babysitter. I'll take Toby with me and hopefully we can get it sorted before I start work at lunchtime. I don't want him to be a bother to y'all."

"Duke?" Babs peered at her son.

"Yes, Mama." He turned to Cora. "You can get settled before you start work if you want. Another day won't make that much difference to me, honestly. I'd rather you were organized because that way you'll be happier in your job and we both win." He sipped his coffee. "Less distraction."

"We have so many empty rooms here. Why would you want to go find yourself an apartment?" Babs turned over the bacon, talking over her shoulder.

"I can't stay here. You don't even know me."

Babs turned to her, her tongs held up like a weapon. "Seriously, sugar, you need to relax. We know enough about you to make the offer. This ranch has so many spare rooms and buildings you could take your pick. Ain't that right, son?"

Duke frowned. "I guess it's a good move to begin with. At least for another night until you find your feet."

"I wasn't thinking short-term, son." Babs stared at him, her eyebrows raised.

"You may as well give in now because there's no way you're going to win against Mama." He put down his mug and stared at her. "Why don't you stay here, get used to the job and once you're comfortable, if you still want to move out you can go apartment hunting then."

"I still have to contact the sitter I booked for Toby. She was expecting him yesterday and probably won't be happy we didn't turn up. I wouldn't be surprised if that spot was gone, just like our apartment."

Babs gave her another long look that made her feel like she was making a fuss over nothing. "You call the sitter and make your apologies but leave him be here. I'll keep an eye on the little man and he can help Grandpa. It ain't no bother. I raised a flock of children. Pretty sure I can cope with one little guy without too much fuss."

It might not be a fuss for Babs but Cora hadn't been brought up the same way. She was used to looking out for herself, making her own decision. Sure, it was nice that they were offering to help but letting go of control could get out of hand. She knew that from past experience. And the last thing she needed was the past coming back to bite her.

Especially with her boss being as devastatingly handsome as her violent ex-partner. She wasn't going to get sucked into a relationship because of such a flimsy attraction ever again, and staying here would be playing with fire.

CHAPTER TWO

uke walked Cora through the restaurant, showing her the basics and introducing her to what staff were already on duty. He paused in his journey, rearranged the condiments trolley and held out a couple of half empty sauce bottles to a passing waitress. Without pausing for breath, he picked up a few menus and slotted them into the wooden rack by the cash register and then skipped up the stairs to the office.

"You'll be responsible for all systems and processes—that includes the food ordering, which you'll go over with Rob on a daily basis, as well as the staff hiring and firing, plus doing the weekly rosters, but Clark will do the wages. Okay?"

"Who's Clark?" She ignored the terseness of his voice and followed him down the hallway, past the staffroom and into the office where his phone rang incessantly.

"One of my brothers. He's the family accountant. You sign off on the final hours, send it his way and forget about it."

"Okay. Does he work here too?"

Duke shook his head and picked up the call, holding the phone against his chest. "Nope. He has an office a few streets over. Just fax or email him everything at the end of the week and he'll sort it out. Same as invoices. You approve them and forward them on. We don't have to handle anything financial at all. Makes life so much easier." Duke answered the call. "Hello." He held his hand up for her to wait.

She glanced around the room as he spoke and poked her head into the connecting office. If half the paperwork was dealt with off-site, she could concentrate more on the staff and the restaurant than the books.

Duke hung up. "Where were we?"

Cora turned back to him. "Your brother doing the invoices and wages. I like it."

"Right. I deal with all front of house stuff so you're free to focus on everything else. Bo said that's your forte so I've taken him at his word."

Cora ignored the desire to verbally pat herself on the back. She had the job. All she had to do was fit in and prove herself. "Got it. And the daily takings?"

Duke put a hand on her arm and nodded to the door she'd just been standing in front of. "Check out your office while I explain."

She walked over to the desk, devoid of any personal touches, and placed her hand on the back of the chair pulling it out. Cora sat down, testing out the seat and peeked through the drawers while she waited for him to continue talking.

"The safe is in my office. I'll show you how that works later when we do a safe drop. It's a two-person job, which we'll go through then. I like the register emptied at least three times a day. After the lunch crowd, the early dinner crowd and again at closing. Everything comes up to the office via an automatic chute so nobody is walking around with a bag of cash, waiting to get pounced on. You do the first two safe deposits up here with the door locked and I'll do the last one before I leave at night. You'll be responsible for letting the security guards in to collect the cash every day at eleven a.m. Last thing I want is the staff to be doing runs to the bank and this is working out for us. Safety is my biggest concern and I refuse to compromise on my workers lives for money." He perched on the edge of her desk. "I don't want to put any of my staff at risk, ever. Most people pay via card these days but there's still a lot of cash floating around. Especially at the bar."

"Got it." She fully agreed with him. Bo had the same system.

"Think you'll like it here, Cora?"

"I do." She bit her lip, expecting him to shout her down much like Babs had done. Not that she didn't appreciate it— she did. But nobody had ever taken over her life like this and it was a little daunting. "But listen, your mom."

He roared with laughter, taking her by surprise.

"What?" Cora smiled. He was a different person when he let his guard down and wasn't in full on work mode. Much like the guy she shared coffee with this morning at the ranch.

He sighed and wiped his hand over his neck, giving her a

massive smile. "Please don't worry. Mama is in her element. She loves having people to fuss over. Gives all us kids a break and that's how we like it."

"All us kids. How many of you are there?"

"Eight all up. Seven boys and one very spoilt sister."

Her mouth dropped open. She had enough trouble looking after one child. She couldn't imagine how Babs did it. "Eight. In that case, she doesn't need me and Toby getting in the way. I can get an apartment this week, Duke. Honestly, it's not a problem." Her mind started to compartmentalize her days so she could fit in apartment hunting and child care. She didn't start till eleven most mornings. That gave her a good few hours to apartment hunt beforehand—once she found someone else to care for Toby of course. How would she do that? Ugh!

He cleared his throat. "No, calm down. I can see in your eyes the way you're already moved out and are sleeping in that damned car of yours. Look, I'm being selfish, but if you don't have to worry about Toby, you'll be able to focus on taking over the running of this place. To be honest, I'm ready for a break so if you stay at the ranch for a while, you'll be doing everyone a favor, me included."

"Are you just saying that so I don't upset your mom?"

He stared at her, the smile gone. "I'm serious, Cora. I may as well be upfront with you. There're a couple of reasons I'd like you to stay and let Toby hang out with Mama and Grandpa. You'll find out soon enough anyway. Mama misses her only grandson and Toby will be a distraction that she needs. So you'd really be doing the whole family a huge favor if you let her play grandma to him."

"Oh, I'm so sorry. Have they moved away from town?"

"My brother, Adam, who you'll meet eventually, divorced his wife, was given custody but she stole the boy and ran. So far we've had no luck getting him back."

"We? Why not get a PI or the police to track her down?"

"I've tried. The whole family has stepped up to help at some stage. We've all put out feelers via social media and drawn a blank. The police are still working the case although they've had no sightings and the private investigator we hired hasn't had any luck either. She's very good at hiding."

"I expect she would be if she's on the run."

"We have no idea where to go from here. It's like we've all run out of ideas." He rubbed a hand over his neck. "She was a friend of mine from college who I brought home one day, and she and Adam hit it off right away. I know how she thinks, what she would do. I promised I'd try and find them for him so he can see his son but so far—nothing." He gave her a rueful smile. "Like I said, Mama needs the distraction."

"Your poor brother."

"I know. As you can see, though, we could use a little young blood around the place." He winked. "Here's a thought. The ranch is huge and we employ a heap of hands. Some live local, some stay on the ranch in cottages or the bunk house."

She raised an eyebrow. Where was this going?

"I happen to know there are always a few empty cottages. You could have one of them if you like. Pretty sure Dad won't mind."

"Seriously?" Sounded way too easy to her. Could she

afford a cottage versus an apartment? "I'd need to know how much it costs before I could give it any thought."

Duke shrugged. "Sure, I'll ask Dad to work it out. And that way Toby could spend time at the ranch with Mama and Grandpa. Everyone wins."

CHAPTER THREE

"**D**ad, hey. How's it going?" He leaned back in his chair and listened to his father's slow Texas drawl booming back at him over the phone.

"Well now, things are pretty good, son. How's that young lady going? Found her feet yet?"

He was yet to meet Cora but Mama would've told him all about her. "She seems to know what she's doing. Gave her a tour of the restaurant and she liked what she saw. Came up with a couple of ideas I hadn't thought of to streamline the kitchen side of things. Nothing huge but useful all the same. Seems Bo had some good ideas in his restaurant that would fit in here. I just hope she likes it enough to stay and turns out to be as reliable as Bo said she was." Duke put his feet up on the edge of his desk and looked at his comfy old cowboy boots. They could do with a polish. Now he had help he might have the time. Something that had been missing in the last couple of years. "Not exactly off to a good start though." He really needed someone to take the weight off his shoulders, and he hoped Cora would be that person.

"Don't see why she wouldn't, son. Just give her a chance. You run a nice place." His father's chuckle came over the phone and his voice softened. "Her young fella is a bundle of energy. Running Grandpa around like a little tornado. Had to send them back up to the house to your mama. I got dizzy watching him."

"He is pretty full of energy. Listen, that's what I wanted to talk to you about. Are any of the cottages empty right now?"

"A couple, maybe three. Why? What're ya thinking?"

"Cora. She had an apartment organized to move into but it fell down when she had car trouble on the way here and didn't make it in time to sign the paperwork. I like having her at the ranch because she doesn't have to worry about Toby. Mama said she's more than happy to look out for him until Cora sorts something out. Daycare or something. I thought, if she could rent a cottage, it would solve one problem off my mind."

"One problem? Son, is there something you aren't telling us? About the restaurant?"

He rested his head back and closed his eyes. Time to come clean with his father. "I have to slow down. Doc is worried about my blood pressure. Claims I'm working too hard and need more down time without the stress."

A curse came over the phone. "Your mama was right. She told me something was up. Why didn't you say so?" A few more mumbled curses followed and Duke waited patiently for his father to blow off steam and come back to the discussion. "Of course she can stay in one of the cottages and don't even think of charging her rent neither. Tell her it's part of her wage package or something, I don't care. They don't cost us anything. What I do care about is my son looking after his health."

"I'm fine. Honestly, it's not that big a deal." At least, that as what he hoped.

"Bullshit. If Doc is concerned, then there's a reason for it. You're not twenty years old anymore. And you do worry too damned much. Always did. Stop trying to have the best restaurant this side of Waco and have a life, son. You never know when it's going to end."

He dropped his feet with a thump. Old! That'd be the day. "I'm not old, and for your information, this restaurant has been holding its own for the last couple of years."

"Good. If that's the case then, you can take a day off and help us on the weekend. A good ride on horseback is probably what you need anyway. It's been a while."

His father's fix-it cure for everything. Duke had to admit, a few hours on the back of a horse worked wonders. Made him forget the real world and all its problems.

"Does your mother know?"

"Not yet. I'll tell her in the morning." But the longer he left it, the longer he wouldn't get hassled over it.

"Make sure you do or I'll be saying something to her myself. You know she's going to freak out over this. Don't be surprised if she sends you to Dallas to a specialist for a second opinion."

"Why do you think I haven't said anything yet?" He wanted the restaurant in good hands before he took any significant time off.

After a few more words of advice, his father hung up and

Duke opened his computer again, adding to the stock list that needed replenishing. He still had to finish all of this, then prep for opening.

His chest tightened.

Stress clamped down on him.

Damn right he didn't have time to see a specialist. Especially when a niggle in the back of his mind told him that his stress levels may have been more than just overwork.

Duke clicked on his history tab and then deleted the page as soon as it loaded. He didn't need to read the symptoms of heart disease again. The symptoms that mirrored his own.

He knew every single word - by heart.

Cora started with the basics. The first thing she wanted to cover was staff contracts because without happy staff, a good restaurant would still fail. Even though Duke had been operating for four years, didn't mean she couldn't find some room for improvement.

She went over the staff contracts and made alterations to what Duke had already set up. It cleared up any shady areas around annual leave, sick days and time off for mental health days and personal reasons. All standard benefits that hadn't been drawn up the way Cora liked. She was a stickler for wording. That took her most of the morning. By the time the lunch crowd had all gone, she had a rough draft ready to show Duke.

Next on her list was safety and first aid. She grabbed a

pen and notepad and did a slower walk of the restaurant, making special care to note everything in the kitchen area.

Rob, the barbeque chef, stood over the hot coals, keeping an eye on his ribs and brisket. "Finding your feet, Cora?

"I am, thank you." She sniffed the smoke as he threw on another large brisket. "That is amazing. The smell is just, wow! What're you basting it with?"

He grinned. "Duke's mama's recipe."

"Really?"

Rob dropped the brush back in his tub of sauce and grinned, a glimmer of humor in his eyes. "Her cooking was what made him want to open a restaurant in the first place. Didn't he tell you that?"

Cora tried to pick out the ingredients from the smell but was hopelessly lost in the kitchen. Chili, garlic maybe but that was it. "Seeing her kitchen at the ranch, it makes sense."

"Now, you didn't come down here to talk to me about recipes. What can I do for you, Cora?" He wiped his hands on the apron around his waist.

"I'm doing a revamp of the first aid and safety in the restaurant and want to make sure everything is as good as it can be." She glanced around looking for the first aid kit. "I don't like getting caught out when it's all too late, y'all know what I mean?"

Rob pointed to a box under the prep counter. "First aid box is there. Duke keeps it pretty well stocked."

"Okay, that's good. I'm hoping there's one in the bar and the restaurant too."

"Yes, ma'am. There sure is."

"What about fire blankets? I don't see one anywhere near your grill." She tapped her pen against her lips.

"Fire extinguisher over there. That oughta do it."

Maybe, but she'd rather not chance it. Better to be over the top than barely getting by in a fire. She was pedantic on safety, a trait Bo didn't have an issue with. "Sorry, Rob. Not in my books. I'll order some. I want one on a wall beside every grill, every hotplate. Doesn't take long for things to get out of hand in a kitchen, especially when people panic. How long since your last fire drill?"

"Don't rightly know." He brushed his sides of brisket again, avoiding looking at her in the eye.

"Have you ever actually done a fire drill in here?" She already knew the answer before he shrugged. Easy to overlook but vital as far as she was concerned. "Okay. I'll organize that too and appoint someone to oversee regular drills. No, you know what? I'll do them myself since I'm the one insisting on this."

"You really are going to whip us into shape, aren't you?" He stared at her, hands on hips. The guy was huge but she didn't feel the slightest bit intimidated. She had a feeling he was a big softie at heart.

"I sure am. That's what Duke pays me for. He has this restaurant running well and he's built up a great name for himself. I want to make sure that the staff are all safe and happy to keep it that way."

"Fair enough. Does that mean y'all be looking at workers contracts too?"

She tilted her head to one side and smiled. "I spent most of the morning doing just that. Something you want to discuss with me, Rob?"

"Yeah. Seems a bit petty but the last place I worked at, they gave the staff a meal. You know, the ones that worked through dinnertime. I'm pretty sure Duke would if we asked him but he's always so busy, don't want to get in his way, you know? Man's been working himself into the ground to get this place as good as it is. He has enough to think about without us staff bitching about a feed." He paused and stared at her. "Maybe you can get Duke to cut his hours back too and stop micro-managing every damned thing. Before he kills himself."

"I'm onto it. If there's anything you need or want, Rob, I want you to come to me, okay? I'm the manager now and my job is to make sure you and the rest of the staff are happy and the restaurant runs well. That way we all make money." She made a note on her page. "The last place I worked at gave the staff meals. Seemed fair to me and I'm happy to implement that here. Who's got the time to whip something up?"

He scratched his chin and sighed. "Guess it'll have to be me. I spend more time in the kitchen standing watching over my grill than anyone else. So long as it's not fussy food, I can do it. Doesn't take much effort to cook up a bowl of pasta or throw a salad together."

"Great. Give me a couple of ideas so I can cost it for Duke and we'll go from there."

She wasn't sure how Duke would take it but she needed to shake things up. There was a lot of work ahead of her—but she was up for the challenge.

Her son was counting on it.

CHAPTER FOUR

Cora stared at Babs and Jack Snr across the kitchen island. "No. Thank you but no." She tried not to see the swiftly disappointment in Duke's mother's eyes and focused on the coffee cup in front of her. "We agreed to a day or so until I found my feet but what you're proposing is out of the question. I need to make my own arrangements for Toby." She'd only been working for two days but getting outside care for her son was still at the top of her list. Cora wished she was anywhere else other than in Bab's kitchen right now. She could hardly walk out when her breakfast was sizzling on the stove. That would be plain rude.

Jack Snr. put a hand on his wife's arm and spoke up. "You'd be doing this family a favor if you did, Cora. I know you don't really know us and you might think you're imposing and we're trying to take over your life but that's not the truth. Babs is happy looking after Toby. So is my father. I haven't seen that much life in him since, well, for ages at any rate."

"Toby needs to go to nursery school. Mix with kids his own age." Cora tried to focus on the spice jars hanging on the wall beside the stove and not Bab's sad eyes in case she lost her determination. She failed miserably.

"I understand that but what's the hurry? Boy has plenty of time to get a school room education. He'll learn lots here on the ranch just like my boys did, and he's safe here too. Not much happens around this place that I don't know about. The hands like him, he's not a bother and he seems to be enjoying himself."

It was true. Last night when she got home from work, he'd had his dinner thanks to Babs. Cora put him in the bath and all he could talk about was the kittens he'd made friends with in the barn, how Grandpa had let him feed the calf and what he had planned for tomorrow. Her suggestion of day care was cried down and Toby went to bed sulking thinking he wasn't going to be allowed to hang out with his new friends anymore.

"I can't impose on you like that. You barely know me but I want you to know I do appreciate the offer."

Jack put his arm around Babs shoulders and pulled her close, a worried look on his face. "Can I be frank with you, Cora?"

"Sure." She was hardly in a position to say anything else nor would she be so rude especially as she was living in this man's house. She settled back in the bar stool and listened.

"Our boy has been burning the candle at both ends getting this restaurant of his up and going. We want him to slow down a bit before he makes himself sick. That's the reason you've got a job. It's all becoming too much for him. He's forgotten how to have fun like he used to. Goes to work every day without the smile he used to wear." He stroked his moustache. "I don't like seeing my son that unhappy, Cora and I'm not above asking you to help put that smile back on his face."

Babs tightened her lips and a flicker of fear washed over her eyes.

"The thing is, if you're taking care of the place, there's gonna be times when you're going to be late home. Goes with the territory, I guess. Last thing you need to be worrying about is what's happening to your boy or if you're going to get a call from the day care to come get him, leaving the restaurant when you're busy. You follow me?"

Cora nodded. It made sense but she still didn't like it.

"I know Duke talked to you about the empty cottages on the ranch and this is what's promoted this conversation. They're nothing fancy but more than livable. We offer them to any of the hands that need somewhere to stay but most of them are happy in the bunk houses for now. They like the companionship of bunking with others. All we're doing is extending that same courtesy to you. It'd make your life and ours a whole lot easier if you say yes."

"Mama, mama, look what I got." Toby came running into the kitchen, a bucket in his hands, leaving dirty marks on the kitchen floor where he stepped.

"Oh, baby. You should've taken off your boots before you came inside. You know the rules."

Babs waved a hand, a smile on her face as she and Jack moved as one toward Toby. "Don't worry about it, Cora. Don't you think this floor has seen more than its share of dirt? This house is lived in, not some fancy display home."

To Cora, it was the nicest home she'd ever been in and

would look right at place on the front of a *Country Life* magazine.

Jack Snr. peered over Toby's shoulder. "Where on earth did you find those, young man? I thought we collected all the eggs this morning." He crouched down and smiled into her son's face. Toby glowed with pride.

"Behind the hay where the tractor's parked. Grandpa said he saw a sneaky chicken in there the other day and I should go a hunting." He grinned, satisfaction lighting his face.

"Well, I never. That's some haul." He ruffled Toby's hair and stood up. "He's happy here and we'd love to have you stay, Cora. It's been too long since a child's laughter has been heard in this house."

Babs moved over to her and put a hand on her arm. "Please say yes, sugar. I miss having a young one around." Tears shimmered in her eyes. How hard it would be to lose access to your grandchild?

Footsteps sounded behind her. "You may as well give in now because I can assure you that Mama will hound you until you agree." Duke plopped himself down on the bar stool beside her and leaned on the counter. His face was pale, eyes red with lack of sleep. What his father said was true, she couldn't deny it.

"What time did you come in last night, son?" Jack frowned at his son.

Duke wiped a hand over his face and screwed up his nose. "Hmm, I think it was about one. Something like that. I had paperwork to sign off on."

"You need to slow down, Duke. You've done too many hours for too long. I worry about you." Babs poured him a coffee and slid it over the counter top. "You've got to let go of some things and let Cora do her job. That's what you employed her for. Don't go micro managing the poor girl when you know she's more than capable of doing her job."

Cora didn't really want to have this discussion in front of his parents but they seemed to know exactly what Duke was doing. Rob had told her as much yesterday. He was concerned about the way Duke was running himself ragged working such long hours.

"He's not so much as micro-managing me as he is going over my work. That's right, isn't it?" She'd noticed her paperwork had been moved when she went into the office yesterday and suspected Duke was double checking everything. Understandable but unnecessary.

Duke nodded.

"And was everything in order?"

He smiled sheepishly. "Yeah. You seem to know what you're doing. I'm impressed with your style. Everything was neat and precise. Worded well."

"Thanks. So now you know it's not necessary to go over everything I do, right?"

He shrugged and took a sip of coffee, avoiding her gaze like a little boy that had been caught out cheating.

Cora shared a glance with Babs and made a decision. These people had given her a new start. One she was eternally grateful for even though she hated being forced into a position she hadn't been prepared for. But even she could see the benefits of what they were proposing. "I'll make a deal with you. You cut back your hours and let me do the job you hired me for. You've already seen me working and you have Bo's recommendation or you wouldn't have taken me sight unseen. I'll stay on the ranch and Toby can too. At least for now."

Duke took another sip of his coffee and then looked her in the eye. "You're giving me the ultimatum? I thought I was the boss here."

She shrugged. Three sets of eyes burned into her face but Cora stood up for herself. She'd come a long way to take up this job and if it meant a little bit of give and take on both sides, so be it. Nobody said it was permanent.

"I'm your manager and you need to let me do what you hired me for. This isn't about your wounded pride or letting go of control. It's about what's best for everyone involved." She ignored the snigger from Jack and continued, keeping her focus on Duke. "If I have to give, then so do you."

He stared at her, his eyebrow raised.

"I'm good at my job so how about you let me do it? I don't need y'all looking over my shoulder." She straightened her shoulders. "No point me being here if you're going to follow me around making me second guess every decision I make."

"Looks like you met your match, sugar." Babs laughed and pulled a heavy skillet down from the rack above her oversized stove. She turned on the gas and started pulling food from the refrigerator.

Cora held her breath, trying to appear nonchalant while she waited for Duke to reply.

"Scrambled eggs with your bacon, Cora?"

"Thank you. That'd be perfect."

"Okay. You got a deal." He leaned back in his stool and crossed his arms. "You tell me when I can show my face and we'll see how it goes. Bet you'll be begging me to come in early sooner or later."

She smiled and shook her head, tried to hide the nerves pinging around in her chest. This was what she was good at, so why was her heart beating so fast? Over the last two days, she'd met all the staff, heard all they had to say about their jobs and knew what she had to work on. Duke's micro-managing was the biggest issue that had come up. Understandable because it was his business but after being open for three years, the place didn't need him there all the time.

"Awesome. You can come in at, shall we say eleven-thirty-ish for the lunch crowd and stay until the bar closes. Once you put the takings in the safe after the dinner rush, there's no need for you to hang around. I want you out of the restaurant by ten at night. Everyone knows their job and obviously they do it well because they're still employed. Security can make sure the place is locked up once the last staff member has left. It's part of their contract—I checked it. You don't need to do that. Everyone knows what they're doing, including me."

His lips twitched and he shared a glance with his father. Casually, he sipped his coffee while he got his words straight in his mind. Bo was right. Cora knew her job. If she had the balls to tell him what to do, his restaurant was going to be fine. "Deal." He turned and held out his hand. After a couple of seconds, Cora put her hand in his and he tightened his fingers over hers. She had soft warm skin and his breathe caught in his throat. There hadn't been time for women in the last few years. Maybe now he could give dating some thought.

He quickly shook that notion away. Not with Cora. The last thing he needed to do was screw up this working relationship when so much was at stake.

His parents share a glance and Duke dropped her hand. "Dad, maybe get Ella to have a quick look at one of the cottages and tidy it up some before you let Cora and Toby in there. Heaven knows what state they're in. Probably home to all sorts of critters."

Cora opened her mouth as if to protest but his dad was onto it already. "Thought crossed my mind. I'll call her later."

"Why isn't she at home anyway? I haven't seen her for ages."

His mom put a plate of breakfast in front of him and Cora. "She's staying in the apartment in town and doing a fabric's course at Baylor University."

He shook his head. "When isn't she doing a course? Isn't it about time she found a real job instead of being a permanent student?" His sister flitted through life like there wasn't any rush to make her own way.

"She is." Babs folded her tea towel and put it on the counter top. "Decided on a business. Ella wants to open her own shop and sell homewares and offer decorating advice. She's good at it, got a fine eye for detail. Once this course is done, I think she'll settle down. Least we hope so, don't we?" She shared a glance with her husband.

Cora spoke up. "I can clean the cottage myself. Don't go

worrying her if she's busy. Toby and I aren't afraid of hard work."

Babs stood with one hand on her hip and the skillet in the other. "She's due home for the weekend anyway so don't fuss, Cora. She enjoys putting things together. Besides, it saves her running riot in my kitchen. She keeps wanting to redecorate and I love things how they are." Babs put the pan down and lifted Toby up on a stool beside his mother. "Now, what can I get you for breakfast, young man?"

He pushed the bucket of eggs in her direction before glancing at his mother. "Please, can I have these?"

Babs took the eggs and gave it careful consideration. "Now, how would you like them? Scrambled, sunny side up, with bacon or as pancakes?"

Toby clapped his hands. "Pancakes. Please."

Cora finished her eggs and pushed her plate away. "I'd better get dressed and head into work." She glanced at Duke. "I'll see you at eleven-thirty—no earlier now, mind." She got off the stool and touched Toby on the back. "Behave, young man. I'll see you before I go." She walked out of the kitchen and ran up the stairs. Moments later her bedroom door closed.

His father laughed. "That's telling you, son. But you employed her so I guess you have to go along with her decisions." He caught the warning look in his father's eye. Jack Snr put his arm around his mom's shoulders and kissed her brow. "Best we make that cottage nice and comfortable for Cora and Toby. I'll give Ella a call and get her geared up to decorate the cottage on the weekend. Girl owes me a favor or six."

His mama rolled her eyes. "What's she gone and

wheedled out of you now, Jack? I swear, you're way too soft with that girl."

"Nothing that I wasn't willing to give. Don't be too hard on her, sweetheart. She'll find her feet soon and make us all proud."

Mama kissed his father and then pushed him out of the kitchen. "Go look after your workers and leave me to my kitchen." She winked at Duke who held back a laugh at the way she bossed his father. "I'll send young Toby down to Grandpa after he's finished his pancakes."

When he was out the door she turned to Duke. "Right, sugar, tell me what's going on."

He looked down lest she see the truth in his eyes. "Nothing, Mama. Everything is going to be just fine."

She leaned on the kitchen counter and stared at him until he lifted his gaze to meet hers. "Don't lie to me, Duke Wilson. Your father knows something I don't and *you* know how unhappy that kind of thing makes me. Now either you tell me or I'll have to take it out on him later when nobody's around to save him."

She would too. Then his father would bitch at him for the next couple of weeks.

"You don't play fair, Mama."

She gave him a coy smile and batted her dark lashes. "Don't know what you're talking about."

No matter how much he disagreed with his mom about that statement, it was hard to be angry at her. She only had his best interests at heart but he was hoping to keep this from her a little bit longer. She'd go overboard trying to make things better.

"My blood pressure is up, energy levels are dropping

rapidly and I'm exhausted but I didn't want you worrying about it. So," he sucked in a big breath, "I employed Cora to take over some of the everyday duties for me. I'm going to be spending less time at the restaurant. Focus more on being the front man and not having to worry about doing everything like I have been since the day we opened." He waited for the tirade he expected at his announcement.

"About time you came to your senses. Not sure how much longer I could've held my tongue the way you've been running yourself ragged, Duke. Seeing you coming home at all hours and going back out again without a decent night's sleep." She dropped a kiss on his cheek and patted him on the back. "Make sure you look after Cora then. Don't want that girl feeling like she has to step up and do everything and get scared off. She has a child to look after as well." She glanced at the young boy busy drawing on the notepad she'd given him while his breakfast cooked. She studied his drawing and dropped a quick kiss on his blond locks. The smile on her face hit him in the gut. He hadn't seen her this happy for a long time.

"I know, Mama. I didn't know that when I hired her." Toby was a shock to him but things were working out fine, thankfully. He was a cute kid and brought so much happiness to this house. Who was he to make judgement on the way Cora lived her life? Besides, Toby was getting under his skin too – in a good way.

"Shouldn't have made much difference as far as I'm concerned. Doesn't make her any less capable and now Toby is staying on the ranch, she'll have less to fret over."

Toby licked his lips and peered over at Duke. "Duke, can you please help me draw a horse? I'm not real good at them."

"Sure, I can. Listen, go into the front room and get a magazine from the table beside the fireplace. We can use that as a starting point."

Toby grinned and clambered down from his stool. He whooped as he ran out of the kitchen.

"He's a great little kid, Duke. It'd break my heart if Cora decided to leave."

Duke wanted her to stay too. Not just for the fact that she was saving him work and taking away the stress that'd been getting him down, but something in her attitude when she started bossing him around intrigued him.

She was a strong, independent woman and that impressed him. He wanted to get to know her better. Find out what made her tick and where Toby's father was. She didn't wear a wedding ring but that didn't necessarily mean anything. The fact that she hadn't mentioned a partner made him want to hear her story.

Toby hurried back in and threw a glossy magazine up on the island before scrambling back onto his stool. He passed a colored pencil to Duke and they started on their joint drawing.

After breakfast, Duke called his sister.

"Daddy already called me, brother. Of course I'll come decorate for you."

"Thanks. I really want this to be special for Cora and Toby. I want her to feel at home."

"Are you trying to tell me something's going on between y'all? About time you thought of something other than that restaurant. Makes a cold bed fellow if you know what I mean?" Ella giggled.

"Don't even go there, Ella. I want her happy at home so

she doesn't have to worry while she's at work. I like my staff content."

His sister snorted. "Sounds to me like you're more invested in her wellbeing than any of your other staff. Don't recall you taking that much interest in Rob's life."

"What? No, you're reading something into it that isn't there. Plain and simple, I don't want to have to hire another manager, okay? And Mama is in love with young Toby. I can't go breaking her heart." He scoffed as he hung up the phone and placed it on his bedside. But as he settled into the chair to do some accounting work from his laptop – what Cora didn't know couldn't hurt her – he couldn't help but worry.

Was he getting too involved in Cora's life?

CHAPTER FIVE

"Today is all about me and you, Toby. How about you show me what you've been up to all week?"

Pottering around the kitchen with her son by her side was like a breath of fresh air. She felt guilty leaving her baby with other people.

"Okay." He frowned. "Does that mean I can't spend the day with Grandpa and the animals?"

He was so settled here already it made her heart ache. He must have been desperate for friends in Santa Fe and she never even noticed. Bad mother point right there. Thank goodness she had agreed to stay on the ranch.

"Tell you what, how about you spend the morning with me and maybe after lunch, if he's not busy, you can go and spend some time with Grandpa?"

Babs put a cup of coffee in front of her. "Sugar, he's no bother. And Grandpa works every day so it won't worry him. Toby has lots he can be doing, but showing his mama around is just the thing for a lazy Sunday, ain't that right, young man?"

He nodded vigorously and spooned in the last of his pancakes. "Yep."

When breakfast was over, Cora took his hand and walked with him down toward the barn. They passed the cottage and she glanced at it. Moving in wouldn't be a hardship even though she'd protested in the beginning. It made sense and as much as she wanted to go and help Ella, she'd been banned from doing anything other than a spot of cleaning before heading into work.

"I want it to be a surprise, Cora." Ella pushed her out the door yesterday with instructions not to come back and sneak a peek until Monday morning before she left for work. Cora stole a glance through the window and quickly turned away lest Ella saw her.

"How is your calf?"

Toby skipped beside her, let go of her hand to pick up a stone that he rolled around in his palm. "Good. Adam said I'm gonna get more. It happens that way, he said. 'Specially with first timers, whatever that is."

"That'll be first time mothers." Duke climbed over the fence and dropped to the ground. A young horse followed and leaned over the top rail. He patted it before joining Cora and Toby on their walk down to the barn. "Always get a handful of orphans and it's good that young Toby here is such a keen worker. I bet Adam appreciates that."

"I'm sure he does." She lifted her face to the sun. "What a glorious day."

Duke tipped his hat back and agreed. "Nothing like it. Wouldn't live anywhere else." He pointed to the pasture over behind the big house. Dark shapes moved amongst the long green grass. "Did I tell you that all the beef we sell in the restaurant comes from the ranch?"

"I think Bo mentioned it. It must make you proud."

"Yes, ma'am. Every single rib comes from the best we can grow. Our stock is well looked after. I believe that's what's made the restaurant so popular. We can trace every single steak we put on the table."

Toby glanced up at him. "You can tell what their names is?"

Cora shivered. Once you named an animal, it didn't go on the menu.

Duke laughed and ruffled her son's hair. "Not quite, little cowboy. We can trace the animal by its ear tag. These beef cattle have a good life and I feel that shows in the quality of the meat."

"It probably does too. Rob mentioned something about it showing on the plate. He'd know what he was talking about and it does smell pretty good."

"You'll have to take Toby in one night for dinner. How would you like that, Toby?"

He shrugged. "Okay, I guess. Can we bring Grandpa too?"

Duke laughed. "Young man, you can bring the whole family if you like. It would be nice if your mama had a night being a guest instead of a worker at the restaurant." He touched her arm. "What do you think, Cora? Would you like to join us all for dinner one night?"

She glanced at him, her heart starting to thud. *Get a grip, girl. He asked you and the whole family to dinner. Nothing special. Calm yourself down.*

"Sounds wonderful." She touched Toby's shoulder. "We'd

better make the most of our day together. See you around, Duke. And thanks." They walked into the dark cavernous barn and Toby headed straight to the pen where the orphan calf bellowed its hunger.

"You got here just in time, Toby." Grandpa walked up with a calf bottle in his hand. "This young 'un was about to come looking for you."

"Sorry, Grandpa. I held him up." Duke walked in behind Cora, climbed up on the side of the pen and slung a leg over, resting his butt on the top rail, then held his hand out for her to join him.

She leaned over the rail and stared at the calf. "Thanks but I'll stay down here." She put her hand through the timber slats and stroked the silky soft ears before the calf charged Toby at the gate and latched onto the teat.

"Doing a great job there, Toby. Ain't that right, Grandpa?"

"He sure is, Duke. This young fella is turning into a real cowboy like it was natural to him."

Cora kept her eyes on her son, aware of the gaze that burned into her head. The sooner he left for work and was out of her space, the better she would feel. At home in his own environment, time spent with Duke seemed too personal. It made her question the logic of staying on the ranch.

The following day, Ella dragged Cora down to the cottage before she left for work. She'd been dying to see what Duke's sister had done to the place.

"This is so cute." They walked in through the front door

straight into a small living room that was open to a pocket sized kitchen. "Wow, what an amazing job you've done." When she'd first looked at the cottage during the week, it was basic but doable if not dusty and unloved. Now it was a pretty little cottage, tastefully but not overly decorated that screamed welcome home to her. "This is so cute."

"Thanks." Ella bounded in beside her and waved her arms around. "I didn't need to do much. Just add a few touches to make it more homely like for y'all. Daddy said you didn't have any furniture so I figured this was the better cottage for the two of you. The others are a bit sparse for you and Toby, probably way too small anyway. I got a few pieces from a friend in town who owns an antique shop and the rest of the items were in the storage shed. I love old recycled things that I can work with. Gives a house more of a homely vibe, you know what I mean?" She grinned and Cora found it hard not to feel drawn to her.

"The hands don't mind not having fancy bits and pieces —not that Adam would let me loose in the bunk house in case I upset his men but I figured I should go all out for you. Make it really pretty and feminine." Ella straightened the vintage wall-hanging by the front door, smoothing out the tassels on the Texas flag tapestry.

"That's so sweet of you." Cora walked over to the little breakfast nook and ran her hand over the table top. A mason jar of Texas bluebonnets sat in the middle for a feminine touch Cora appreciated. Cushions softened the wooden u-shaped seat with splashes of the same violet blue as the flowers picked from the pasture.

"Come in here and look at what I did to the bedrooms." Ella grabbed her arm and dragged Cora into the next room off of the living room. A queen sized bed sat in the middle under the window, with barely enough space to walk either side of it. Ella had placed slim night stands with mismatched lamps with blue shades which gave the room a charming country look. The same light blue was splashed across the abstract framed print above the bed.

"And this here is young Toby's room." Ella guided her into the living room and through to the other bedroom.

The single room had been decked out with her little boy in mind. A wave of appreciation swamped Cora. A white bookcase filled with children's books sat under the single window. Pressed up against the wall was an old wrought iron bed. The quilt looked handmade and worn but still in excellent condition. A shelf loaded with stuffed toys was within easy reach for those special cuddles at night and a lamp hung over the end of the bed with a pull switch fit for a child.

"That quilt was made by our grandmother. She loved to sew. I think I got some of her genes because I'm the only one that really likes to decorate. Mama got the cooking genes and sadly that passed me by. I gotta make do with what I have."

Cora would be happy with either of those traits. Sadly she had neither. She was an organizer, a doer. "You've done such a beautiful job, Ella. Thank you so much. I seriously wouldn't know where to start if someone told me to decorate."

"You're welcome. Duke was very specific about what I did for this cottage. Are you and my brother...?"

"No!" The words were out before she could think. Cora was stunned Ella thought that way. She'd only been in

Wishbone for a little while. "No. We're work colleagues, nothing more." Where on earth did that idea come from?

"Sure thing." Ella grinned and toyed with her long curly hair. "So, when are y'all moving in?"

"I wish I had time to do it now but Toby has the contents of our suitcases scattered all over the room. Sunday is my normal day off, so I guess that'll do unless I get an early mark from Duke. We don't have much so it'll make things that much easier."

"I can give you hand if you want to move in earlier. I'll be here in the morning but heading back to Baylor University after lunch to catch up on some study. I have a paper to prepare."

"You don't have to do that. You've already done so much and I really do appreciate it."

"Think nothing of it. When Daddy hollers, 'jump to it, girl,' I do exactly as he says. Let me know. It won't take us long." She opened the pantry door and showed Cora the contents. Jars lined the shelves, labelled and full of ingredients. "Mama is determined you stay here so don't go getting all proper and upset if you see her loading up your refrigerator or cupboards. She lives to cook and feeding everyone is her favorite thing to do apart from trying to rule us kids. It's her Creole and Louisiana heritage or so she claims. I'm surprised she isn't head chef at the restaurant to be honest."

"That's not necessary, honestly. How can I stop her?" This was becoming embarrassing and she hadn't even moved in yet.

"If I was you, I'd give up trying before you start. Just let her do her thing and she might eventually calm down.

Besides, if she's fussing over you, I get a break." Ella laughed. "Nothing like having your mama rock up to college with enough food to feed an army. Anyone would think I can't fend for myself." She brushed her hair from her face and shut the cupboard door. "Well, that about does the guided tour. Guess I'd better let you get to work and do your thing."

Cora glanced at her watch. "Yes, you're right. Time I left. Thanks once again. It's way more than I deserve."

Ella made a dismissive noise. "Anyone that can put up with my brother deserves a medal."

Now it was Cora's turn to laugh. "He's not that bad. A bit overworked maybe but perhaps with my help, it can only get better."

Ella turned her cornflower blue eyes to Cora, a look of wonder spreading across her face. "He's really letting you take charge and tell him what to do?"

"Not exactly tell him what to do but I'm the restaurant manager so I get to run the place as I see fit. Duke is going to slow down and be more the front person because everyone wants to see him. He's the face of the restaurant and that's what he should be concentrating on, not the mechanics of the business."

"I hear you told him that too." She shook her head, her dark curls bobbing around her face. "Guess he likes you better than you think."

No! The last thing Cora needed was a man in her life apart from her son. She didn't need or want the complication.

Not after what she'd left behind.

～

"Join us for an early bite to eat, Duke." Rob poked at his brisket, brushed it over with sauce and nodded his approval. "Made turkey subs today. Your mama's sauce on 'em."

"Is it working out alright, giving the staff a meal?" He couldn't believe he hadn't thought of it. That was one massive brain fade on his part. Thank goodness for Cora. He'd been so focused on the customers and producing what they wanted, he'd dropped the ball as far as his staff were concerned. But they'd stuck with him, which he considered a miracle.

"Sure is. Boosted morale, which is always a good thing. I mean, some of them don't want to eat but most manage to grab a quick bite at least. Keeps them happy and energy levels up. I don't mind doing it."

"Good. And thanks, I'd like that." He took the plate Rob offered and pulled up a stool at the other end of the prep table. "Listen, I wanted to talk to you anyway about something we've spoken about before. I was thinking of selling Mama's sauces now I'm going to have more time on my hands to market them. She keeps hinting at it and I don't have any reason not to do what she wants." He took a bite of his turkey sub and chewed for a moment before continuing. "Now, I'm not asking you to prepare them or anything like that. I'm happy to have them made off site. My question is, do you think they'll sell?"

"Hell yes but I already told you that. I'd buy it by the box, man. But aren't you supposed to be slowing down, not ramping up the business?"

Duke frowned. "Who told you that?"

Rob laughed and slapped Duke on the back. "Man, you should see your face. Chill out, dude. I've known you since high school. I got your back."

"Cora?" Telling everyone his business wasn't part of her job. They might have to have a serious chat about what was appropriate and what wasn't. That was if he was brave enough to take her on. Duke suspected it would be a bit like arguing with his mama. He wouldn't have a hope of winning.

Rob shook his head, picked up his sub, inspected it and then spoke. "Nope. Your mama was in yesterday early. Wanted to give me a box of chilies she picked from her garden and she made noises about us making her sauces. Wants to know what's holding us up."

Cora got a pass. Duke grinned. "She has a soft spot for you—always has. I bet she wished one of us kids cooked like you do."

Rob chewed, nodding in agreement. "You got it right there. I'll be happy to stick to being an honorary Wilson though. So long as she keeps bringing me gifts like yesterday, that is." He put his sub down, wiped the back of his hand over his mouth and leaned on his elbows. "But listen. Do you really want to take on something else right now? Why not wait a bit and get your health under control and then revisit the idea. I don't want your mama coming down on me if you get sick."

Duke looked at his hands, inspecting his nails rather than looking in his friends face. He felt well, most of the time. But he felt something else too. Angsty and agitated. As if he wasn't doing enough. Just the thought of slowing down was making him second guess everything he did. "I find it hard to sit still and do nothing."

Rob wiped his hands and pushed his plate away. "What does the doctor say?"

"Not a word of this to Mama, understood?"

"Sure."

"Blood pressures up, heart racing and I need to slow down before I have a stroke or a heart attack. He blames my crazy work schedule and that's why I hired Cora." He wasn't ready to mention his real fears, even to his best friend.

"She's good at her job. The staff like her."

"That's great but now I feel out of sorts. Do you have any idea what it's like to not be able to come into work at my normal hour? I had to go for a walk to kill time so Mama and Cora wouldn't kick my butt. Adam's gonna give me a job if I hang around the ranch much more. I even helped Ella move Cora's belongings into the cottage so she didn't have to do it on the weekend." He wiped a spot of mayonnaise from the edge of the plate and licked his finger clean. "I feel like I'm stuck behind a wall of glass and I can't find the damned door back into my real life."

Rob laughed and shook his head. "Man, you need to learn to relax some. It's only been a week or so, give it time. Before you know what's happened, you'll be used to it."

Doubt it! "You know me. I have to move. I don't know if this is going to work, like things aren't any better for me health wise." He didn't know how to explain it. Kind of like getting a craving for chocolate when you decided to go on a diet. He was craving more work. Crazy.

"Cause you ain't giving it a chance, Duke."

"A week is a good chance in my book."

Rob rolled his eyes. "Did the doc order any tests?"

He hadn't told his parents this much because they'd only freak out at him but speaking to Rob was easy because he knew it wouldn't go any further. His best mate from high school and his head man in the kitchen was a good sounding board. Always had been. "Yeah. I agreed that if things don't calm down, I'd go through the barrage of tests he's asking for. Considering I hate needles, I'm not looking forward to doing it anytime soon so I'm keeping my fingers crossed that it clears up."

"Grow up, pal. Get it done and then you'll know for sure if there's anything to worry about. All you're doing is delaying the inevitable." Trust Rob to try and shame him into doing it. Duke wanted to know if there was something wrong. But at the same time, would it be better to live in denial?

"Tell you what, if you don't go and do it soon, I will have a word in your mama's ear."

The sneaky bastard! Duke glared at him. What he'd done to deserve this from a trusted friend?

Rob shrugged, obviously not worried about what Duke thought. "I'd rather have you pissed at me than dead. I'm telling you that for free." Rob cleared his throat and glanced over Duke's shoulder. "Cora. Hey. What's up?"

CHAPTER SIX

S o that was why she got the job. Duke's health wasn't what it should be. She knew he had to slow down because he'd told her as much but she didn't realize it was as serious as Rob just made out. "So, that bad, hey?" She walked over, leaned on the steel kitchen counter and looked between the two men.

"Nothing to worry about." Duke glared at Rob but the big man held his hands up like he didn't want to be a part of their conversation anymore.

Was that fear in Duke's eyes or was he pissed off she'd heard them talking? "I don't believe that for a minute."

"I'll be fine if I survive those damned needles," he muttered.

She grinned, mischief firing through her veins. How could this big muscly man be afraid of a little needle stick? "Want me to go with you and hold your hand? I've had practice with that since I'm a mom and all." Her lips twitched at the sight of twin spots of color highlighting his very handsome cheeks.

Annoyance flared in his eyes. "Thanks but I have it under control."

Boy did he sound pissed. But Cora didn't care. It took more than a grumpy man to put a dent in her happy. And for the first time in ages, she was starting to feel relaxed again.

She wasn't about to let anything get her down now she was in Wishbone. In the short time she'd been working at the restaurant and living at the ranch, she'd become quite attached to the family. All of them. One more than the others. If something happened to Duke, it wouldn't be good. She'd stir him all she could if it meant he took care of himself. "I somehow doubt that. But since you're the boss, and its personal, I'll leave it. What I came down for was to put the new roster on the board. A couple of staff members requested time off so I juggled the shifts." She smiled at Rob. "If you have any issues with it, give me a shout, Rob."

"Sure. No worries."

She turned away, pinned the roster up and then headed back to her office. Was there anything she could do to help encourage Duke to undergo the tests his doctor wanted. She liked him more than she'd intended. Not just as an employer but as a man. He was kind and gentle. He talked to his staff like a friend and didn't come off as better than them just because he was the boss. He treated her son like one of the family. Something she appreciated and would repay him for in spades.

Customers loved him. If it wasn't for Duke being the face of the restaurant, she doubted it would be quite as popular. There were plenty of barbeque restaurants in Texas. Heck, it was the beef capital of America but not everyone could claim the turnover that Duke's place had.

She'd gone online and checked it out when Bo told her about the place.

Cora walked back to her office, pausing at the outside bar to make sure everything was running smoothly. The restaurant buzzed with the chatter of diners. "Hi Nelly. Need anything out here?"

The barmaid was pulling a tray of beers. "Nope. All good thanks." She put the last glass on the try and one of the girls picked it up and scurried away with it. "Listen, Cora. Do you think I can change my shift next week? I need some personal time."

"Is there someone you can swap with?"

"Yeah, Leo said he'd do mine if that was okay by you." She wiped the bar down with a damp cloth.

Cora smiled. "Sure thing. The roster is inside with Rob in the kitchen. I only just put it up so if you could go and make the adjustment, that's fine. And if there's anything we can do for you, shout out, okay?"

"Appreciate it. Thanks." A staff member breezed past, handed over a docket with another order and Cora left her to it and headed back to the office.

Duke stood at her desk when she walked in, hands on his hips and a frown on his face. He must have high tailed it to beat her up here.

"Hey."

"Hey. Listen, I didn't mean to snap at you down there. It's just that this is playing on my mind and I'm a little bit tense about it."

Cora slid into her chair giving him a gentle smile. "Don't worry about it. It'll take more than you being scared of getting blood tests to upset my day. You forget, I have a toddler and boy, can he be stubborn when the mood takes him."

Duke's lips twitched at the edges and laughter danced in his eyes. "Are you trying to suggest that I'm acting like a child?"

She blew out a breath. "Seriously? Maybe. If the shoe fits, slip that baby on and pull those laces tight."

He burst out laughing and ended up having a coughing fit. "Sorry but that was too much."

She leaned back in her chair. "Thanks. Look, I'm not trying to tell you what to do because that wouldn't be appropriate but I care about your family already. You've all taken me under your wing and it wouldn't do for me to not return the effort. If you need help, personal or workwise, feel free to call on me. I don't mind. And as I said, I'm used to dealing with toddlers tantrums so you being a bit scared of facing the truth won't worry me at all."

He leaned over her desk. "You're right. When it comes me and my health, I'm a big wuss. Pretty sure things will calm down once I ease up on things. At least that's the plan."

"I heard you talking about your mom's recipes. Did you want me to have a look and see if we can find an industrial kitchen to give a quote to make them for you? Or did you want to employ someone in house to do it?"

Duke pulled over a chair and sat down. "I'm not sure. I hadn't really given it much thought, to be honest. I mean, I eat it every day at home and we serve it here. People are always asking for t-shirts and mugs and other brand stuff and so far we've managed to keep customers happy. I thought asking Rob was the best way to gauge interest because we've danced around the idea before but the timing was all wrong. I've had people ask for it lately and so far I've had to turn them down but it's something that's been in the back of my mind for a while now."

"You two go way back, I hear?"

"Yeah, we do. High school, then college. Both Wishbone boys who couldn't bear to be away from our hometown longer than necessary."

"I might chat to Rob more, see if he's interested in overseeing someone to do it here, then. It makes sense to keep things in house so long as we don't overload the staff."

"Hire more if you want to. But we need to make sure it's going to be profitable first. No point in losing money."

She laughed. "Not going to happen on my watch. Didn't Bo tell you I was a math whizz? I hate spending more than is necessary."

"To be honest, he sung your praises so much I thought he was joking. Made me wonder why he let you go if you were so good."

The shutters came down over her eyes. He'd said too much.

"Sorry if it's too close to home but since we're talking personal business as well, I have to ask. Is there a Mr. Hamilton?"

"No." She snapped the word out and then bit her lip.

He really was on touchy ground. "Okay. Sorry."

She closed her eyes and looked down at her hands, reminding him of the night he first met her in the parking lot.

"No, I'm sorry. Here I am interfering in your life and being rude when you ask obvious questions." She softened her voice. "I never married Toby's father but he's no longer in the picture. Let's leave it at that."

"That's fine. I wasn't trying to get too personal but I figured there must be something going on for you to hike halfway across the state when you already had a good job."

Cora picked up a pen and started poking it on the daily planner, clicking it off and on. Duke waited, let her work out her words.

"I decided that it was best for me and Toby to move on before he ran out of money and started hitting me up again. He has a habit of causing trouble every time he comes around even though I have sole custody. I was over it and Toby doesn't need to be reminded his father is a good for nothing guy who'd rather run a scam than hold down a decent job and provide for his family."

Cora lifted her chin defiantly but it didn't take away from the vulnerability clouding her eyes. She came across as brave and determined but Duke could still see the loneliness hanging over her. Was that sympathy he felt for her or something else?

"Fair enough too. Don't blame you and I'm glad we got the opportunity to get to know the both of you better. His loss is our gain."

She gave him a shy smile. "Thanks."

"No, I mean it. Mama and Dad are thrilled to have you and Grandpa is having so much fun with Toby at the ranch. Best thing that's happened to him in ages. Given him a whole new lease on life." Duke denied it earlier, now he wasn't so sure. *It's a darned good thing to happen to me too.*

"Toby talks about him all the time. Even as he's struggling to stay awake at night, it's all about Grandpa. He's never had grandparents before so it's all very nice for him."

"You don't have any family?"

She shook her head. "Nope. Just me and Toby these days."

"Well, I guess you found a new tribe then. As you've already noticed, my folks don't feel any sense of shame dragging anyone into our family."

"That's very sweet and I don't want you to think I don't appreciate it but I'm not used to anyone doing so much for me. It feels a bit overwhelming at times."

"Well, you'd better get used to it. It's how my family works. And listen, while we're on my family, I have to ask you something. Grandpa has fallen hard for Toby. He wants to teach him to ride but wanted me to run it past you first. Do you mind?"

"Um, do you think that's a wise move? Doesn't he have other stuff to do that's more important?"

Duke shook his head and sighed. "Cora, Cora. You need to chill out and take what's offered without worrying you're putting anyone out all the time. Grandpa wouldn't have offered if he didn't want to do it. He loves having Toby around and from what I hear, the feeling is mutual."

"But it's a big ask. Learning to ride isn't a five minute job. He needs to learn how to look after the horse as well. They're not something you can put in a paddock and forget. Least that's what I was taught."

Duke leaned forward and grinned. "You ride? Why didn't you say so?"

She blushed and shrugged. "I don't know. Never came up

I guess but this is Texas. Girls learn to ride horses growing up, don't they?"

Duke clapped his hands and laughed. "I suppose so." The color rose on her cheeks and a warm wave of emotion rolled in his stomach. He couldn't be falling for her already, surely?

"Listen. Dad is at me to go out with them on the weekend for a cattle muster. It's his answer to anything that troubles you. Riding a horse is guaranteed to blow away the cobwebs and give you a new perspective on life. He's always ribbing me about not being a proper cowboy because I don't ride enough."

"And that digs at you, right?"

"Yeah. I was born here on the ranch and rode most of my life. Only college and setting up the restaurant has stopped me from sitting astride my horse. As far as I'm concerned I'm a true Texas cowboy even if I don't get out with the herd as much as I used to."

Something flickered across her eyes and Duke swallowed down the apprehension.

"Would you care to join me? I could show you some of the ranch, get you away from the restaurant for a few hours and Sunday is supposed to be your day off. What do you say?" He held his breath.

She seemed torn and indecision flittered across her eyes and she looked away. "If you're sure, I think I'd really like that."

A small shot of joy zipped up his spine. "Good. Great. I can take you closer to those cattle. Then you can honestly say you know where the steaks and ribs come from. See how the cattle are looked after." He should shut up before he said too much but Duke couldn't seem to help himself. "Awesome."

"I haven't been on a horse for years so I hope I don't make a fool of myself."

Duke could picture it – this beautiful woman, legs either side of a horse, smiling in that contagious way she had that was starting to make him lose his mind.

He hoped he didn't make a fool of himself either.

CHAPTER SEVEN

I f anyone looked more at home on a horse, Duke
wanted to see them. Cora sat in the saddle, one hand
holding the reins loosely and the other stroking the
horses mane as he did up his girth strap.

When she'd arrived looking the part, worn jeans, check
shirt and a wide brimmed hat he'd been taken back. Her
boots were scuffed and well-worn making him grin. She
looked like she belonged.

"What?"

"Don't mind me. I had visions of you arriving with a
pressed pair of jeans and a button up work shirt. I didn't
take you for the country girl but I'm pleased to admit, I was
wrong."

A smile twitched her lips. "I can look professional when I
need to, Duke."

"I know that. What surprised me is how relaxed you look
now, how country you are. I'm impressed." He hesitated a
second and then put his arm around her shoulders. "Come
with me; there's someone I want you to meet." He drew her

into the massive big barn. Inside were stables, most of them empty because the horses were already outside being saddled up.

He came to a halt in front of a stable where a palomino had its head hanging over the door. Duke rubbed her ears and she closed her eyes. "This here is Buttercup. She's Mama's horse but she rarely rides these days. Such a gentle old girl. You won't have any problems with her."

"She's gorgeous." Cora held her hand out and got a sniff and snort for her troubles. "Hey, beautiful girl."

Duke opened the door, clipped on a lead rope and led her out. "I can help you saddle her if you like."

"No, let me. Pretty sure I remember how to do it." She took the lead rope and tied it to the loop already outside the stall. "I gather the saddles are in there?" She pointed to a tack room, the shelves of blue, navy and forest green folded blankets visible through the gap in the door.

"Yes. Let me show you which saddle is for Buttercup." He ignored the looks he got from the ranch hands and walked into the tack room, grabbed a hand tooled western saddle and nodded at the bridle above it. "You grab that. Saddle blankets are there." He indicated with his chin to the shelf where stacks of blankets were ready for use.

Cora followed him back to the horse. He put the saddle over the door. "Right, all yours. Let me know if you need anything. I'll get my horse." He strode off, passing his father on the way.

"Hey, Cora, Duke."

"Good morning." The rest of the conversation was lost in the noise of the barn. His horse snorted when he opened the door, frisky that he hadn't been ridden for some time.

"Settle down, big fella. Settle down." Duke clipped on his lead and brought him out. "Time for a big ride, what do you say?"

He led him back to Cora who was pulling the belly cinch tight while his father looked on.

"This little lady knows her way around a horse, Duke. You didn't tell me that."

"I didn't know myself until midweek when I invited her." He glanced over the saddle and bridle and gave a nod. "You haven't forgotten how to do it."

Cora grinned. "No. I thought I would but once I breathed in that familiar stable smell, it all came back to me. I'm really looking forward to this ride. It's been years since I was on a horse."

Jack Snr smiled. "I'm guessing young Toby has your genes then. He has a way with animals and Grandpa is pretty excited to be teaching a young'un to ride again."

"About that." Cora rubbed her hands on her jeans. "I don't want to impose on…

His father held up his hand. "Now just you wait a minute, Cora. I know what you're going to say and I want to put a stop to it right now. You're not putting anyone out, interfering with anyone's routine. Let me make that clear." He smiled to soften his words.

"I know you already said that but I still feel like I'm imposing. I'm sorry to go on about it but..

"Then don't." A tall dark haired cowboy stopped beside them. "Take it with the gratitude it's given with."

Duke put a hand on her shoulder. "Cora, meet my brother Adam. Adam, this is Cora. She manages the restaurant now."

"Nice to meet you, Cora and welcome to the ranch. Word around is that you're good at what you do. Everyone appreciates that and your little guy is pretty amusing too."

She blushed. It seemed to Duke that Cora wasn't big on praise. "Thanks. So long as he doesn't get in the way."

"Not likely with Mama and Grandpa overseeing things. Now, if y'all are ready, I'm about to head out. Hope you're prepared for a big ride, Cora. We have to go to one of the outer pastures and round up the steers. Bringing them in can be a challenge and while I don't expect you to tag along all the way, it's still going to be a big day. This isn't a job for sissies."

She lifted her chin. "I might not have been on a horse for a few years but I'm pretty sure I can cut it with the rest of the team."

Adam tipped his hat. "Right, let's go." Then he walked away.

"Is he in a pissy mood or what?"

"Don't go getting stirred up, Duke. It's Daniel's birthday today and he's bitter and sad all rolled into one. Don't blame him none, either. We all miss that little guy."

Cora sighed. "It must be hard."

She understood Adam more than anyone knew. She'd been bone-achingly terrified when her ex-boyfriend had taken Toby and tried to run. She shuddered remembering the fight, the blood and her sons terrified screams. Having the police rock up and place her under arrest hadn't helped matters at all.

She pushed back the memories, content to leave them hidden from view. She worked better when she didn't hang onto drama or painful thoughts.

"Breaks all our hearts." Jack Snr wiped a hand over his chin.

Cora put an arm around his shoulders and gave him a quick hug.

"I get it, truly I do. I just didn't want to be a bother to anyone."

Jack Snr returned the hug, his voice hoarse with emotion. "Never a bother. Get that through your head, young lady." He cleared his throat. "Right, let's get going before Adam has a melt-down. He'll have a schedule and I don't want to go ruining his day any more than it already is."

Cora climbed on the gentle horse and shuffled her butt around in the saddle until she felt comfortable. It felt good to be on horseback again. How long had it been? About eight or nine years, long before she had Toby anyway.

"Ready?" Duke rode up to her, his horse sniffing and rubbing heads with hers.

"I sure am. I'm really looking forward to this. Thank you so much for asking me along."

Duke gave her a lopsided and way too cute grin that sent warm waves to her belly. "I don't expect you to work every single day, Cora. You're allowed down time or you'll burn out. That's the last thing I want."

"Like you?" This morning he still had black rings around his eyes. So much for him slowing down now she was the manager. "I don't mind the extra hours if it helps you."

"Appreciated. I'm probably still doing too much but I'm getting there, okay? It's in my DNA to be an over achiever.

Today is the first time I've been out with the guys for almost a year. That's gotta be a good sign."

He looked so earnest that she had to smile. "True."

Duke lifted the reins and nudged his horse forward. "Follow me and be prepared to be wowed. The pastures are looking amazing right now. At least that's what Dad keeps telling me."

Cora followed him out of the barn, and took a deep breath of clean country air. Oh, she'd been enjoying the peace since she woke up this morning but there was something to be said for seeing the world from the back of a horse. It had a way of draining all of the angst from you and giving you a sense of calm.

At least that was the way she was going to look at it for now. That niggling twinge in the middle of her shoulder blades could wait for another day. If there was anything coming to upset the balance she'd fought so hard for, Cora was ready to do battle and protect what she had.

CHAPTER EIGHT

"Let's stop for a breather." Duke pulled up beside her as they made their way into another pasture and a stock hand pushed the gate back as he'd done all along the ride. "Adam and the boys are only going to the back of this pasture and will bring the cattle in to this point to push them toward home, so we can wait here and stretch our legs if you like."

She smiled and loosened the reins. "You know, I hate to admit it but I could do with a break. My butt is feeling this."

They'd only been on horseback for a little under two hours and he was feeling it in places he'd forgotten he had. "Me too and I was born to this so don't go feeling like you've let the side down." He tipped his head to a large low hanging tree near the fence. "That looks like the perfect spot to catch our breath and take in the view."

He turned his horse in the direction and Cora followed at a leisurely pace. Duke dismounted and threw the reins over his horses head. He knew it wouldn't go far, preferring to munch on the rich green grass this end of the pasture where there were no cattle.

Bright purple flowers poked their heads throughout the pasture. Spring was his favorite time of year when the bluebonnets brought color to the plains and everything took on a fresh new look.

Duke believed in fresh starts and with Cora here to help run the restaurant, he finally felt as though he was at a crossroads looking at a bright future. He could have his restaurant without the stress that'd been dogging him since he opened the doors and that feeling gave him a sense of hope for the future.

Cora pulled up beside him, threw a leg over the saddle and slid to the ground.

"That's one way of dismounting."

"I always was a bit of a rebel." She tipped her hat back and smiled, her gaze roaming over the pasture. "This is perfect, Duke. Absolutely perfect."

"I know. I struggle to find the time to come out here because of the restaurant and I always make excuses but now I'm here, it makes me wonder why. This is the best part of living in Texas. The wide open pastures, the riot of color that comes with spring and the fresh smell of sunshine."

She glanced at him, a soft smile on her face. "You're looking better too now we're out here. More relaxed than I've seen you."

Was she flirting with him? No, he was being silly. He'd taken an innocent comment and turned it into something suggestive. "Guess you're working your charm, Cora. I appreciate you driving all the way across the state to manage things for me." *Work for me, not flirt with me. Keep things in perspective, Duke.*

"I needed a change and you gave me the chance. I reckon that makes us even, don't you?"

He shrugged. "Maybe." Duke took his hat off and dropped it on the ground near the base of the tree so the horses wouldn't stand on it. He ran his hand through his hair, the soft breeze cooling his scalp.

"I bet Bo was sad to see you go?"

She smiled. "He's a good man. Gave me the chance when I needed it. I miss him and his wife. They were good to me and Toby."

"He couldn't sing your praises enough. I have to say, at first I was doubtful. I mean, if you were that good, why would he let you leave?"

"I told you why."

"You did and that's not what I was getting at. What I'm trying to say, Cora, is that I'm glad you're here. Glad your circumstances brought you out to this place." Glader than he realized, now he'd had time to think about it. Would she think the same way if the opportunity arose?

"Thanks. I appreciate it." She turned and watched the ranch hands in the distance spreading out to bring in the cattle. "This is nice being outside. It's not a wonder Toby loves it here so much." She held the reins in her hand loosely as her horse dipped its head and grabbed a tuft of grass, chewing contentedly.

"He's one very special little man. Mama adores him already. He's snuck into her heart at just the right time."

She smiled before looking serious. "Listen, tell me to mind my own business but any more news of Adam's son?"

As soon as the words were out of her mouth, Cora regretted it. This was too close to home and she didn't really want to go there again. Her own memories were still too painful to unpack but something about the sadness in Adam's eyes pulled at her. Made her wish she could do something about it so he had his son where he belonged.

Duke took the reins out of her hand and threw them over her horses neck. "She won't go far." He took her hand and led her to the shade of the tree. "Sit down and rest a bit. It's nice here."

Cora tucked her legs under herself and sat down, leaning her back against the tree, the rough bark digging into her back.

Duke frowned. "Nothing yet. After Daniel was born, Lissa started on antidepressants which turned into substance abuse and that was what messed up their marriage in the first place. It broke his heart to take it to court and the family tried to help her plenty before he took that step. She didn't want to help herself. Thought we were all trying to take over her life." He pulled a stem of grass and stuck it between his lips. "I lost count of the times we got her into rehab. She'd come out and we'd think it was all fine but it never was. She was a master at deception. Eventually we all ran out of the will to try."

"That's sad for y'all." Cora ran her fingers over the soft petals of the blue bonnets.

"Yeah. I felt so bad about introducing her to Adam in the

beginning. If it wasn't for me, he wouldn't be going through hell now."

"He didn't have to marry her. I think that was his choice, not yours."

"Perhaps. Anyway, she decided she didn't want to be married anymore. She kept taking off, leaving Daniel behind. It got to be that he didn't want to know her when she came back begging for another chance and Adam would give it to her hoping that this time she'd stick but it never happened."

"It's hard to let go of a dream when you love someone." She gave him a quick smile. "I should know. I loved Toby's father once. But that was before I realized what he was really like."

"I thought I knew her too but I was wrong. She fooled all of us. But not the judge. He gave custody to Adam, much to her dismay. So she took him on a court appointed visit and ran."

"How long ago was that?"

"Going on two years. We've had people actively looking for her but not a sign of either of them, not anywhere."

"Poor Adam."

"Yeah. So you can see why Mama is so in love with Toby. It hit us all hard. But we haven't given up hope."

"You said your brother is the sheriff. What does he say?"

Duke bit the end off of the grass and chewed it before answering. "Clay has all the appropriate alerts out but nothing he can do unless someone comes forward with a sighting. He suggested a private investigator and we did that too but nothing so far."

"I'm really sorry."

"You're very sweet, Cora. Thank you. It means a lot that you understand and care."

"I understand more than you know." She closed her mouth before she could say too much. She'd dealt with everything that had happened on her own and still struggled to put it into words. Cora glanced at Duke, her cheeks heating at the intense gaze on his face. Her lips parted and she blinked. Why was he having this effect on her? She turned away.

Duke reached over and cupped her chin in his hand, turning her back to face him. "I hope you don't mind but I want to kiss you. If you don't want me to, say so."

Her heart pounded but she found it hard to move away from him. Something about Duke tugged at her heartstrings and she had no idea what it was.

His lips touched hers, the softness surprising her. Cora leaned into him, placing a hand on his chest as they explored the sensations rising between them. She wasn't ready for a relationship. At least that was what she told herself. Her body had other ideas.

The ground trembled beneath them, and they broke apart. Cora held her hand over her heart. "That was intense."

Duke laughed. "I wish I had that much effect on you but I have to admit that wasn't me making the ground move for you." He tipped his head in the direction the ranch hands, his father and his brother went. "They're headed back."

Cora glanced up. A hazy cloud drifted over the horizon. The cattle were coming closer. Her cheeks heated and she stood, wiping her hands over her jeans in case there were tell-tale signs of grass on her that would give away what they were just doing. Not that it was a crime to sit under a tree and kiss a handsome man but she wasn't here for a relationship. She was here for a job. Cora didn't want anyone to get the wrong idea, especially Duke.

"Don't be embarrassed, Cora."

She held her hands to her hot cheeks. "I'm not." Liar, liar, pants on fire. He made more of an impression than she wanted. But she couldn't act upon her feelings. Not with her boss. It wasn't right. "It can't happen again, Duke. I came here for a job, not a relationship."

She strode over to the horse and calmed herself by gathering the reins and mounting up again. She could do this, act as though he didn't affect her. She had no choice if she wanted to stay here.

She hadn't felt this safe in years. Nothing was going to ruin that for her. Certainly not her emotions.

Cora managed to act normal the rest of the day and spent a quiet night in with Toby having dinner together for the first time this week and then snuggling on the couch watching a family movie. He was exhausted from the riding lesson Grandpa had given him and it didn't take much to get him into bed that night. He was asleep before she walked out of the bedroom.

Unlike her, who tossed and turned all night. When she woke the following morning, her greatest fear was facing Duke at work and feeling embarrassed. She had to stop this from getting blown out of proportion. There wasn't time for a relationship with Duke or anyone else. It wasn't in her plans. What if it went wrong? He held her entire future in his hands. She worked for him, lived on the family ranch and relied on his family for babysitting. She'd used her entire savings and come clear across the state to take up this job. Duke could take away everything from her if their relationship turned sour. She couldn't risk it. Not until she knew her and Toby were in the clear. And that wasn't likely to happen any time soon.

CHAPTER NINE

Cora managed to get through to almost lunch time on Monday without running into Duke.

He walked into her office with a smile on his face. "Thought you might like these." He dropped a file on her desk and pulled up a chair.

"Thanks. What is it?"

"Some new products we think we could use. It's getting to be big business selling goods out the front of restaurants. Customers love the t-shirts the staff wear and the stubby coolers sell well too. Anything connected to the restaurant seems to be working so I found a few other things that we might be able to put our logo on and use. Let me know what you think."

"Sure." She opened the file. "Listen, about yesterday."

He held up a hand. "Wait, I don't want you feeling awkward. It was a kiss, nothing more. Admittedly a very nice kiss but if it makes you uncomfortable, I'm sorry."

She gave him a quick smile. "It's just that…"

"You don't want to date the boss?"

"Well, if you put it like that, yeah."

Duke burst out laughing and Cora almost felt silly for worrying about it. His laughter turned to a groan of pain and he held his hands to his chest. "Duke. What is it?"

He paled as he stared at her. "Tight. Oh my god, that hurts." He screwed his face up.

She reached for him, and he slumped onto her desk.

Oh God no. What was happening? Was it his heart?

She forced herself to move. *Grab the phone. Call an ambulance.*

Cora dialed and waited for the call to go through.

Dukes eyes fluttered; his body trembled.

Answer the damned phone. Hurry up.

Duke slid from the chair and landed on the floor, unconscious.

What should she do? Hang up? Give him CPR?

A woman answered and Cora told her the situation.

"Ma'am, I want you to put the phone on speaker and start CPR. Can you do that?"

"Yes." She hit the speaker button, dropped the phone on the desk and fell to her knees. "Duke, stay with me. Help is on the way."

"Talk to me, ma'am. I'm not going anywhere. I'll stay with you until the ambulance arrives."

"I think he's breathing." Cora kept her hands on his chest, doing compressions.

"That's good. Don't stop yet though. Let's keep him stable until the paramedics arrive. They should be there any minute. You're doing well."

Duke moaned and Cora almost fainted in relief. Seconds later, the wail of the ambulance pierced the air.

An hour later, she paced the hospital waiting room, desperate for an answer but nobody seemed to know what was going on. Rob had texted her so many times to find out if there was any news. It only added to her fears.

He'd insisted that she followed the ambulance so Duke had someone with him when he regained consciousness. Not that he'd had to tell her twice. She was just about ready to scream in frustration and ask the poor overworked receptionist once again when a nurse walked out of the emergency room and put a reassuring hand on her arm. "He's fine. Doctor is with him now. You can come through if you like now we have him stable."

Cora followed her through the door and into the cubicle where Duke lay back, wires going from his chest to the machine beside his bed that registered the results on a screen overhead. She didn't begin to understand the jagged lines and continuous beeps.

He gave her a sheepish grin when he spotted her and her stomach dived. "Sorry to freak you out like that."

Cora put one hand on his arm thankful he was alive and talking. She'd lost years off her life waiting to hear him speak again. "Are you alright? What did the doctor say?"

The doctor walked in at that moment. "The doctor says this man is in need of a rest. His blood pressure is through the roof and after discussing it with his doctor, we've agreed the only course open to us is to put him on medication and rest. Lots of rest."

Cora grabbed his hand and squeezed it tight. There was a connection between them, despite her earlier insistence that it wasn't possible. She'd have to tread warily. "So he's going to be alright?"

"If he does as he's told, yes." The doctor wrote a note on his file. "Stress does a lot to a body. Like this episode. It can be frightening and if not dealt with; things can get out of control. Luckily this time it wasn't serious but that's not to say that one day it won't be."

A deep sigh escaped her lips. "Thank goodness. I wasn't looking forward to telling your mom."

His jaw dropped. "You didn't call her did you?"

Cora shook her head. "No. Almost but the doctors said it wasn't a matter of life or death, and that you'd be okay. I wanted to get some idea of what was wrong before I upset them."

Duke blew out a breath. "Thank you. Mama will have a fit when she finds out."

The doctor stood beside him, watching the machine above his head. "First thing I want you to do is take a week off and let the medication do its job. No work, just rest. Stress is one of the biggest causes of high blood pressure and if you don't get it under control, you could have a stroke or a heart attack. If you need more than a week, take it." Duke gave a nod and the doctor continued. "I'm giving you a script for a drug that should help settle your blood pressure."

"Thank you."

The doctor glanced between them. "But there are other things you can do yourself. You can cut fat and salt out of your diet, exercise more, and I can't say it enough - lose the stress, Duke."

"Mediation and yoga help, don't they?" asked Cora.

"They do. Also cutting back on sugar and refined carbs too. Your doctor and I both agree you should have those tests now. We want to eliminate kidney problems, diabetes and high cholesterol while we're at it. He said you don't have that kind of family history but you never know. You can book them in on your way out and if you have any more problems, don't hesitate to call him or come and see me."

"So, I'm good to go then?" Duke sat up and swung his legs over the bed.

"Yes, you are. Fill this and get those tests done." Duke took it, patted his pocket and gave Cora a sheepish glance. "Could you hang onto this for a minute? I don't even have my wallet."

Cora took the script and put it in her handbag. "Sure, don't worry. I can get it filled for you later if you like."

She helped Duke with his shirt and held him upright as he faltered on his feet.

"Wow, bit wobbly there." He grinned and leaned against her. Cora breathed in the woodsy aftershave he favored and enjoyed the warmth of his body on hers. It would be easy to make something of this but he'd brushed off her apologies earlier, saying that their kiss meant nothing.

Good, she wasn't that interested anyway. She was better sticking to her guns about a relationship regardless of how tempting it might be. And right now the temptation was ramping up.

She steadied him and moved back putting distance between them. "Okay now?"

"Yeah, thanks."

When Duke was ready, she slid her arm through his and she walked him through the hospital. They made appointments for his tests and then headed out to the parking lot. "My vehicle is over there."

"Thank you. You have no idea how much I appreciate what you did."

She shrugged. "For what? Anyone would've done it."

"For not calling my folks. Mama is going to go crazy." He held his hand above his eyes to shade the sun.

"Moms tend to do that when they worry about their kids. Goes with the territory." Cora clicked the automatic door lock and helped Duke into the truck.

"Yeah, I guess." He did up his seat belt and Cora got in the driver's seat.

"Now, your next move. I can drop you at home or you can call your dad to pick you up from work. Your call."

He gave her a shaky laugh. "I'm good to drive myself. Take me back to the restaurant."

She snorted and shook her head as she pulled out onto the road. "Nice try. Nope, you're not driving until you get this script filled and have a couple of days off. I'll stop at the pharmacy and then take you home if you like. Your truck will be fine locked up at night."

"I need to do the close of the restaurant."

She rolled her eyes at him and turned onto the highway. "Not this week, you won't. You heard the doctor. One week of doing nothing, maybe more. That starts now, not tomorrow." She smiled to soften her words. "I'll manage. I'm just going to have to rely on your mom to deal with Toby." As much as she didn't like to do it, Cora had no choice. Her job was important and if she couldn't help Duke out when he needed it, she didn't deserve to be his manager.

He remained silent until they got back to the road the ranch was on. "Listen, pull over for a second, will you?"

Cora did as he asked. Duke turned in his seat and faced her, a frown on his face. "I'm not sure how Mama will react but I'm thinking it's going to be bad. Can we just tell her I didn't feel well and leave out the hospital visit for now? I'll tell her the truth later."

"Promise?"

His eyebrows drew together as he thought about it. "Yeah, I promise. Thing is, she's going to freak out seeing me driven home as it is. Don't want to go pushing my luck."

Cora tilted her head to one side and smiled at him. "A word of advice from a mom. Tell her now. There's no good reason not to. Get it over and done with in one hit." She took his hand and squeezed his fingers. "If it were me, I'd prefer it all up front. Better that way than two hits, if you know what I mean."

"You don't know her like I do."

Cora smiled. "But I'm probably as ferociously protective as she is. Just tell her, Duke. If you're that worried, call ahead and ask your dad to meet you at the house. He can run interference and keep her calm."

Aray of light shone in what would otherwise be a dark day. Boy, she was good at coming up with ideas. Duke grinned. "Good idea. I like how you think." He pulled his cell from his pocket and called his father. "Hey, Dad.

Listen, somethings going on and I need your help." He told him what had happened and was pleased to hear his father agree to meet him at the house. "Thanks, Dad. Be there in ten minutes."

Cora smiled as he hung up. "Thank you."

"What for? I should be thanking you for all you're doing." He slid the phone in his pocket.

"Thank you for being kind to your mom. She'll appreciate it."

"She's going to kill me. I can feel it."

Cora laughed at him. "Toughen up, princess. You have her wrapped around your little finger. I've seen the way she dotes on you."

He snorted. "Only because my brothers aren't all there for her to annoy."

"Where are they? You said you have six of them. I've only seen one so far."

"Yes, Adam. Well, Clark is in town as I said. You'll meet him one day soon, I'd imagine. Guy loves numbers better than anything." He grinned. "Adam manages the ranch as you know but don't be surprised if you don't see much of him. He tends to keep to himself and bunks down in one of the cottages past the barn. Ever since his divorce, he's gone into a shell. Shame really because he was such a fun loving person before shit went south."

"Sad but I can understand his pain having gone through what I have with Toby's father."

"Yeah. That's why it's so important that we find my nephew. That'll put a smile on his face if nothing else does."

"I wish you all the luck."

"Thanks. Anyway, back to the brothers. My brother

Clay is the sheriff in town, still single much to Mama's disgust. Jack Jnr has a whisky distillery and makes a mighty fine drop even if I say so myself. Single but dating anyone that will have him like he doesn't have a care in the world. Then there's Cody, he works at a small animal practice in Dallas. Mama is at him to come home but so far he's resisted her efforts." He laughed. "Guy is smart. He knows that once he gives in, she'll be on his case to get married and have kids."

"Bit of a matchmaker is she?"

"You have no idea, Cora. Fair warning too. If she starts dropping hints, run like the wind." He glanced out the window. Hopefully his mom wouldn't think of pairing Cora up with any of his brothers but he wouldn't put it past her. Sure, he said that kiss meant nothing but he was lying to himself. It meant more than he could have imagined. "Now you live on the ranch, I wouldn't be surprised if she takes it in her mind to sort you out as well."

Cora turned away from him but not before he saw the blush stain her cheeks. "Like that's going to happen. I have too much on my plate for romance at this time in my life. That was what I was trying to tell you when you went all heart attack kind of crazy on me. All I want is a peaceful existence and a job I enjoy."

A small fire burned in his belly. He wasn't prepared to let go of her that easy regardless of what he said. He might have to ease her into a relationship but not before he gave her a chance to settle down and his health improved. "And how is that working out for you?"

"Good. It's working out great. I love it here and the job is just what I like too."

"Pleased to hear it. I guess we'd better go tell Mama she can watch over me for a week."

"In a minute. You still have one more brother."

He ticked them off on his fingers. "Clay, Adam, Jack, Cody, Eli and Clark. Who did I leave out?"

"Eli."

"Oh right. Sorry. He lives in Dallas. We don't see much of him because he's in demand as an entertainment and sports lawyer."

"You mean like movie stars and sports players?" She turned the ignition on again and started down the driveway to the house.

"Yeah. They call him at all odd hours. Poor guy never gets much time to himself, even on weekends. Don't know why he bothers to be honest."

"Have you ever thought that working yourself to the bone runs in the family?" Cora drove over the cattle grid and onto the driveway that circled in front of the house before she answered. "Or maybe he likes the rock star lifestyle."

He wasn't going to admit to the former. "Maybe he does." Duke put his hand on the door handle when she put her truck in park and turned off the ignition. "Thanks for today. I really do appreciate it. More than I can say." She was good to have around. The more he got to know her, the more he wanted to see where things between them would go. He just had to convince her that it was okay to fall in love with the boss. Somehow, Duke didn't like his chances but he wouldn't be a Wilson boy if he didn't keep trying.

Coming to on the floor of his office with her leaning over him was a shock. So was the fear in her eyes. He'd have to tread warily if he wanted to change Cora's mind about the two of them. Being out of the restaurant for a week perhaps would be the perfect time to try and change her mind about him. *About them.*

Somehow Duke had to convince her that working for the boss wasn't the worst thing in the world.

CHAPTER TEN

"Mama, calm down, please." Duke knew it was pointless as soon as she came out the front door onto the porch and saw Cora helping him out of her truck.

"Don't you go telling me what to do, young man. I'm your mama and I'll do what I do best. Now tell me what's going on. Your father is in the kitchen, pale and stressed busy telling me not to stress out." She put a hand through his arm and helped Cora steady him up the stairs. "Red rag to a bull, saying that. Same as when y'all were in trouble as kids. Always got my back up 'cause I knew right off that you'd done something stupid." She glared at the man in question as he came out onto the porch with an apologetic shrug. Not many people won against his mom. Not even his father.

He ignored the cough coming from Cora but saw the light in her eyes. She found all of this fussing amusing. He would have too if he wasn't the one on the end of it.

"I'm fine. Bit of a scare but as you can see, I'm okay." He

walked inside with the two women holding onto him and found a seat in a comfy old leather chair in the front room. His mom fussed around him puffing up cushions and pushing a stool for his feet before sitting down.

"Right, that's good then." She swallowed. "May as well let me have it, Duke. And don't even think about telling me only half the details either. I want it all and I want it now without you trying to play it down. Understand?"

"Yes ma'am." He shared a glance with Cora who stood by the door watching the commotion.

"If you'll excuse me, I'll go say a quick hello to Toby. Be right back."

She ducked out before he could convince her to stay. If his father couldn't protect him from his mama, what hope did Cora have?

"Wise lady. Spill the dirt, Duke before I get more worried than I need to."

"Mama, don't you go getting all wound up now, I'm okay." He told her everything the doctor said leaving nothing out.

"Just as well you have Cora to look after things. You can rest up and not stress over the restaurant. Sleep in, relax, maybe spend some time enjoying the fresh air on the front porch. It'll do you good, Duke. I've been saying for ages that you're working too hard. That restaurant could just about run itself the way you set it up anyways."

"So you say but it's a living thing, Mama. It changes along with the people that work there. It's not something I can walk away from and ignore if I want it to keep going the way it is."

"It is now you have Cora." She took the medication he

held in his hand. "Let's see what we have here then." She read the instructions and nodded. "Right, I'll get you a coffee and a snack so you can take these and then you're going to rest, young man."

"Yes, ma'am."

She bustled out and Duke stared at his father. "That went better than I thought."

His dad took a chair. "Well, it's like this son. We've both been saying for ages that you're doing too much. It's not like we didn't expect something like this to happen." He wiped his hand over his chin and smiled. "Not that we wanted to see you laid low but we're not that surprised." He leaned over and patted Duke on the leg. "Best thing you did was employ Cora. That little guy of hers is just what this ranch needed too. Grandpa has a new lease on life and your mom is so much happier with him around. Probably half the reason she didn't whoop on your butt now like I thought she would." He sat back and tapped his finger on the wooden part of the arm rest like he did when he was thinking. "She'd make a real good friend, Duke. Cora, I mean. Be kind to her, okay?"

A good friend? That was one way of looking at it. He wanted that and more but was this really the right time for him to be looking at a relationship? He didn't think so although the temptation was there and his heart had other ideas.

They got on well, shared similar interests and were both go-getters. Not that that alone was enough to base a relationship on. But there was also a vulnerability that pulled at him when he looked into her eyes. A past hurt that he felt the need to help heal. He wasn't a knight in shining armor by any means but he was keen to investigate where their friendship could go. That was if working together wasn't going to stuff it up.

Cora walked back through the house and found Duke sitting where she'd left him, his father lounging in the chair opposite. "I need to get back to the restaurant. You'll be okay now?"

He gave her a droll look and it reminded her of Toby when he was being petulant. "Sure. Mama is all over it."

"You got that right, sunshine." Babs waltzed into the living room carrying a tray with coffee and a plate of cake. "You'll be wise to do as you're told and not get too smart mouthed about it either. You haven't done such a good job of looking after yourself lately and look what happened."

Cora smiled, folded her arms and stared at him waiting for another comment.

"I came home and told you the truth, didn't I? What more do you want from me?"

Babs ruffled his hair as if he was four years old and he ducked away but a smile lifted the corners of his lips.

"I want you to do as you're told and get well again. If Cora needs help, she can call one of your brothers or I'll go in. You got that, Cora?"

"Yes, ma'am. I do. Pretty sure I can manage though. Everyone knows what they're doing. If you don't mind keeping an eye on Toby, I can do what needs to be done at the restaurant."

"Now you stop worrying about a thing, sugar. He can

stay in the house with us while you're working late. I'll go down to the cottage and get him a few changes of clothes if that's okay with you and if you don't get back to the ranch by his bedtime, we'll put him in the upstairs room. You can collect him or join us for breakfast in the morning."

"Thank you, Babs. I really appreciate it. Just let me know if he's any trouble, okay?"

"That little boy is no trouble, Cora." Duke's father stood. "Grandpa is a changed man now Toby is here. Fact is, we miss having a young one around so it suits us just fine. You go about your job and don't worry about a thing, now. You hear?"

"Thank you all. It's wonderful to have so much support." It almost brought her to tears. Back in El Paso she had nobody to help out and had to make do on her own. "I'd better get going and do some work before the boss gets antsy." She pointed at Duke. "Be good now, or your mama is going to be telling me all about it and you won't be allowed back at work for longer than the week the doctor said."

He threw his hands up in mock outrage. "Women. Why do they think they have to boss me around?"

His father laughed. "Probably because you need it son. I'd better get back down to the yards too. Boys are bringing in some young steers and I want to check them out before they let them loose again."

"Bye all." Cora waved and walked out to her truck, thankful that Duke had gotten such a good diagnosis. Now it would be all about running the restaurant so well that he didn't stress over it and he could get better. This was a job she had no plan on leaving any time soon so Cora was determined to do the best she could.

She got in her truck and headed back into town. There was a restaurant to run and her warring heart to sort out. Seeing Duke in pain had hit her hard. She didn't want a relationship, especially not with her boss. But her heart may have different ideas. Her only problem was seeing how long she could ignore it and do her job.

CHAPTER ELEVEN

Cora opened her eyes and stretched her arms above her head.

She checked her watch. 8:30. Cora jumped out of bed and dressed in a pair of jeans and a t-shirt. Babs would be wondering where she was. Toby would've been up for ages and was probably running her ragged. He was a bundle of energy in the mornings and no matter how kind they were looking after him, she still felt bad about leaving him for so long.

The smell of bacon and fresh coffee hit her long before she opened the back door of the big house. Laughter came from the kitchen. It sounded as though Toby was entertaining someone. A smile rose on her lips. She'd missed him.

"Hey, everyone. Sorry I slept in." Cora grabbed Toby from behind and smothered his cheek in kisses. "Good morning, sunshine."

He giggled and wriggled out of her arms. "Stop that."

She kissed him more. "No way. I have my goodnight

kisses to make up for." She planted a firm kiss on his forehead before letting him go. "You behaving yourself?"

Babs laughed and placed a mug of steaming coffee on the kitchen island counter for her. "This young man is so well behaved, you don't have to worry about a thing."

"I appreciate it. Thank you."

"This man, on the other hand, is desperate for your company." Duke patted the seat beside him. "I can't begin to tell you how much I miss going into the restaurant. Fill me in. What happened last night? Any issues with orders? What was the nights takings? Any problems with customers or staff?"

"Duke, it's been one day and not even a full one at that." She took the seat and reached for her coffee. That first sip was magical. It energized her as it tickled down her throat and into her belly. A hot coffee, a decent night's sleep, and time when she'd been at work and she wasn't worried about her son – how perfect. There were no issues with the day care. No last minute calls because the after-hours sitter had to leave early. That made all the difference.

She sighed as the caffeine hit her bloodstream and put down the mug.

"You look like you just won the lottery." Babs placed a plate of French toast with a side of mushrooms and bacon in front of her.

Cora's heart melted just a little bit more. "You don't have to feed me."

Babs waved a hand. "Oh, sugar, when're you gonna realize that's what I like to do? Don't want to go upsetting an old lady do you?"

Cora laughed. "Old, you aren't. And I really do

appreciate it. I was just thinking when I walked in that this was the first time I've worked nights without having to stress over what was happening on the home front." She nodded in her son's direction. "It makes all the difference and I don't know how to thank you."

Duke put a hand on her arm and squeezed. "Just so you know, works both ways."

She snorted. "You're kidding me? You're panicking thinking about what you missed out on."

He had the sense to look slightly ashamed and gave her a bashful grin. A grin that was way too sexy first thing in the morning. "Not panicked. Missing out. There's a difference. I feel kind of lost not being there. It's been my life, every single breathing moment just about for the last few years. Kind of hard to take a break from, ya know?"

"Understandable but stop worrying. Everything is fine. We had a good night. Nobody caused any problems, and everyone paid their bill and gave good tips so the staff were happy." She smiled at the picture she had in her mind of the girls sharing out the tips. "Tonight will be busier I think. We have some large parties coming in, birthday and a work celebration but the staff are prepared and I don't foresee any problems." She rattled off the nights takings and other pertinent information he wanted to know before she picked up her knife and fork and started eating.

Cora just accepted another cup of coffee when Grandpa walked into the kitchen with a bundle of fluff tucked into his chest. He glanced at her, gave her a wink and walked up behind Toby who was busy coloring on a notepad Babs had given him, so intent on his picture that he hadn't noticed him walking in the door.

Grandpa coughed and cleared his throat making Toby jump.

"Grandpa. You scared me." He grinned and threw down the coloring pencil and tilted his head. "What do you have there?"

"Well, it's like this, young Toby. One of the hands found this little thing out in the pasture and we have no idea who it belongs to or where it comes from." The tiny orange pup lifted its nose and stared at the humans. "Not sure what I should do with it, you know? Should I take it into town and see if I can find it a home? I need a young man to help me take care of it."

He glanced at Cora and gave her a smile that would melt butter on a cold winters day. He already had her son's heart —right now he'd grabbed a big chunk of hers too. Nobody had ever treated her son like this and she wanted to cry in gratitude. A hand snuck onto her lap from behind and grabbed hers, giving it a quick squeeze before moving away.

Duke rested his chin on his hand and made clicking noises with his tongue. "Gee, Grandpa. You're asking a lot of Toby. He already helps you with the lambs and the calves. He told me he feeds the chickens and collects the eggs too. Do you really think he has time to look after a motherless pup? That's asking a lot of any man in my opinion."

"No, no, no, no. I can do it." Toby shot off his chair and reached for the pup. "Please, Grandpa, let me have him."

"It's a huge responsibility, Toby." Cora didn't for a moment consider saying no when Grandpa had hinted at it the other day although it could make a difference when she eventually came to renting a home in town if that was what she did. She was too happy seeing her little boy excited at having his own pet. "That little guy, gal, can't be left on its own. You need to be really certain that you can take care of it all the time. Animals aren't something you can put down when you get sick of them."

"I won't, Mom. I promise." He held his arms out and Grandpa put the pup into his arms. Toby's face shone and Cora had to fight back the emotion watching him.

"Every child should have a pet." Babs came around the island drying her hands on her apron. "Grandpa, what kind of dog is it?"

"No idea. It's too tiny to be a coyote but I don't understand what a domestic dog would be doing out in the pasture. Looks to me to be a small type breed. That pokey little face reminds me of one of those little poodle type things."

Little black eyes shone out of its ginger face and watched them. A pink tongue whipped out and licked Toby on the hand making him squeal with delight.

"You need to find a name for her, Toby. Something pretty because I reckon she's going to be a very pretty little girl when she grows up. All fluff and sass, that one." Grandpa moved over to an empty chair and sat down.

"I'll think real hard, Grandpa." He gazed at the old man. "Is she really mine? I can keep her forever?"

"That's right. So long as you look after her, she's yours."

Duke stared at his grandfather. There was something going on here that he was missing. He was sure of it. That puppy didn't look like it was neglected or undernourished. It was clean too. Too clean to be a stray someone had found in a pasture.

His mom shared a smile with her father and then bustled around to the other side of the island and pulled open a cupboard. "Let's get that little thing something to eat. I bet she's half starved. Probably hasn't eaten for ages. Looks like skin and bone to me." She put a couple of little bowls on the counter top and stepped over to the refrigerator. "Just as well we have some top quality hamburger in the cooler. Now, Toby, you bring her around here and feed her. We'll only give her a tiny bit to start with then see how she goes. Okay? Don't want to go upsetting that little belly of hers."

"Yes, ma'am."

"How old you think she is, Grandpa?"

Grandpa wiped a hand over his chin, smoothing down the small goatee. "Well now, I reckon she'd be about eight to ten weeks. Not much more. Bit hard to tell really." His left eye twitched.

"Right. Lucky that she's old enough to leave her mother then. Heaven forbid you have another baby that needs bottle feeding."

Grandpa shook his head. "That wouldn't be any bother, Duke. Y'all know that."

Mama passed a bowl of hamburger to Toby who sat down on the floor and put it in front of the little pup. She sniffed it and poked out a tongue to lick it before delicately eating every last morsel. Then she sat on her butt and licked her lips.

"She liked it." Toby grinned. "She must have been hungry.

"I bet she was. By my calculations, she probably didn't eat much since last night."

Cora turned and looked at him, a smile in her eyes.

Duke shrugged. "I'm guessing that's when she got parted from her mother. She's too clean to have been on her own for much longer than that."

Grandpa cleared his throat and turned away. "You may be right. But, thing is, now she has a home with young Toby. No need to worry about a thing anymore, that little girl. No sir, she's going to be fine."

A smile lifted the corners of Cora's lips and she turned away. The silence in the kitchen became heavy with innuendo and his mom looked uncomfortable.

"Grandpa, do you have something down in the barn Toby can use for a bed for this little one? I'm sure Cora would appreciate that."

"Bound to be something down there. I'll take young Toby down later and find something. You alright this pup being an inside dog, Cora? If not, she can sleep in the barn with the big dogs."

"Mom, please? She can sleep with me." Toby picked her up and snuggled her against his neck. "She's too little to sleep in the barn. She'll get lost. I don't mind sharing my bed with her. Please."

Cora laughed at his attempt to convince her but he could have saved his breath. She was a sucker for animals, especially tiny cute ones. "She can but on one condition."

Toby waited, his mouth open.

"If she makes any messes of any kind, it's up to you to deal with it, understand?"

"Yes, ma'am."

"And you need to ask Babs nicely what she wants you to do with the pup when you sleep over here. If it has to stay in the barn, I don't want you sulking to get your own way."

Babs smiled and patted Toby on the shoulder. "We'll see how she goes. We might need to crate her so she doesn't leave little puddles on my good carpet. But when she grows up a bit, we will talk about this again. I don't have a problem with a dog in bed with the child. Okay?"

"Yes, ma'am."

"Toby, how about you come with me to the cottage for a little bit before I go to work? I'd like to spend some time with you." Cora got down off the stool and picked up her empty plate and coffee cup. "We can see how your little girl likes your room."

Babs took the dishes from her. "You don't have to do that."

"I'm capable of putting my own dishes in the dishwasher, Babs. You don't need to wait on me. It doesn't feel right."

"Go on. You know I like looking after y'all. It's what I do best." She stacked the dishes and wiped her hands. "You and Toby go do what you want and we'll see him when you head off to work." She leaned down and stroked the puppy on the head. "I can't wait to hear what you name her, Toby. She's a very pretty little lady."

Cora followed her son out of the kitchen, aware that Duke's gaze followed her. Just one more thing that would make it harder and harder for Cora to walk away. She was getting torn between what her heart wanted and what her brain screamed at her. Which was she going to listen to?

CHAPTER TWELVE

Grandpa got up and shuffled his feet. "Best I get back to work."

"You take care now, you hear, Daddy?"

"Always."

"Wait a minute, Grandpa." Duke stood and followed his grandfather out of the kitchen and onto the back porch. "That pup wasn't a stray, was it?" He glanced skyward. A red-tailed hawk circled over the pasture near the barn. Heaven help any rodents out today.

"Whatever makes you think that, Duke?" Grandpa bashed his hat against his leg and put it on as he walked down the steps into the yard, refusing to admit to anything.

"It was clean and healthy. Not hungry or mistreated. I think you and Mama are planning something and I don't think I should like it."

Grandpa stopped and turned to him, a frown between his bushy gray eyebrows. "Son, you gotta relax. The boy needed a puppy and I was in a position to get him one. Cora didn't seem to mind when I hinted at it during the week. No harm in having another dog on the ranch, is there?"

Duke grinned despite his attempt to stay neutral. Give his grandfather any sign of encouragement and there'd be no stopping him. Only one marriage in a large family, and a failed one at that, was getting to his elders.

He put his hands on his hips and breathed in the clean air, the scent of fresh cut grass coming from the pasture where a tractor made a lazy circle around his mother's fruit trees. The geese honked, flapping their wings to show how much they hated being disturbed and waddled to another shady spot. "There is if Cora decides to move to town. Who says that her rental agent will let her have pets?"

"The pup can stay at the ranch if that's the case. No matter where she ends up, while she's here, Toby needs something he can call his own."

"And you think you're the right person to make that decision on her behalf?"

Grandpa picked a twig from the lavender bush, the perfume floating in the air as he rubbed the leaves between his fingers.

"Wasn't quite like that, son. Babs mentioned to me that Cora said they'd never had a pet because they never had the space. Now they do. Regardless, I don't think that's gonna happen, do you?"

"What do you mean?"

"I've seen the way you look at her, Duke. I may be old but I'm not blind by a long shot. That little lady and her son mean something to you and it's not just that she's a good worker either. A man with half a brain would be silly not to make something of that, if you want my opinion."

"Don't recall asking actually."

His grandfather flicked the lavender twig in the garden bed. "That's the problem. You kids never do and that's why I've decided that y'all need to be prodded now and then. I spent forty-seven years with your darling grandmother and I miss her every day. You need someone to love like that, Duke. Just because Adam had one failed attempt doesn't mean y'all have to avoid relationships."

"We're not." It didn't feel right that it was his grandfather that brought it up. Not that Duke didn't trust his judgement, he did. It was just that having someone see so plainly how he felt made him a little bit uncomfortable. Especially since Cora had said she didn't want a relationship.

"You are. I know it too. Now, what's holding you back if it's not what happened to your bother? I hope it's not that lovely little man of hers."

Nothing could be further from the truth. "No. Don't even think like that. I really like that little boy already, not that I've spent as much time with him as you have. He's adorable." He blew out a breath. "No, it's Cora. The timing's not right." Duke glanced away, embarrassed and hurt that the first woman he'd been interested in in ages wasn't feeling the same way he was.

"Duke, you gotta learn something about people who've experienced bad relationships. They put their guard up, especially ones like Cora who end up alone and the only breadwinner. She has a little guy to take care of and that's her first priority, and I don't blame her in the slightest. Some women don't want to risk their hearts again because it takes too much to recover from. Be kind to her. Show her you care and that she has nothing to be scared of with you."

He put a beefy arm around Duke's shoulders. "You're a good man, Duke. I know you can make this work if you put your mind to it. Take it steady. One step at a time, son."

"Thanks, Grandpa." He gazed down the driveway toward the little cottage Cora lived in. Did he want to share that with her and Toby or was it impossible, given the circumstances? The biggest job he had now was to try and figure that out and not scare her away in the meantime.

Cora drove back to the cottage just after midnight. She turned off the truck engine and sat staring out into the darkness, letting the quiet soothe her. She was exhausted; her feet ached and so did her face from smiling. It wasn't the easiest job in the world being the face of the restaurant and she was keen to leave that to Duke when he felt better. But she was happy. It'd been a good night. The restaurant had been filled to capacity and there'd been no problems apart from the odd slightly tipsy patron stumbling between their table and the bar but they'd been dealt with easily enough.

A tap sounded on the window. She screamed.

Duke jumped back, an apology coming quickly. "Sorry. I didn't mean to scare you."

She held her hand over her racing heart, taking a few deep breaths to calm herself before opening the door. "I was miles away. Is Toby okay?"

Duke grinned and held up a hand. "Yes, he's fine. I heard you come in and was tossing and turning, couldn't sleep. Bit hard to settle with so much on my mind and nothing I can do about it."

Cora grabbed her purse and slid out of the truck, slamming the door behind her, fighting to still her racing heart. "Coffee?"

"If I'm not interrupting you, sure. I didn't mean to put you on the spot. It's just that when I heard the truck coming down the drive I figured we could chat for a few minutes— maybe that would settle me down and I could sleep. But on the same hand, I don't want to keep you awake. You've had a big night." He followed her inside the cottage.

"No problem. I can't go to bed right away anyways. I need to wind down and then I'll sleep." She stretched and rolled the kinks out of her shoulder blades before repeating her offer. "Coffee?"

"Sure but let me do it. You sit down and put your feet up. You deserve the break."

Cora did as he suggested. It was divine to kick off her shoes and relax with her feet up knowing that nobody was going to come through the door and demand her attention. She rested her head back on the couch. Duke pottered around in the tiny kitchen. Soon he had the coffee pot on and the smell hovered in the air. How long had it been since she'd managed to down a full cup? By her calculations, it was just after lunch. Almost twelve hours ago. No wonder she was tired. Her caffeine well was depleted.

He handed her a mug, shuffled the pillow back on the other end of the couch, tucked one leg under the other and sat facing her. "So, how did it go?"

Cora sipped the coffee, letting it trickle down her throat before answering. "Very good night. No problems, lots of compliments too. I was speaking to Rob about your mom and your suggestion that you bottle and sell her sauces. I've been thinking it over and I've come up with some other ideas too."

"Oh, have you just? It's not like you have plenty of spare time."

She smiled and tried not to focus on the dimples in his cheeks when he gave her that huge grin. "I multi-task pretty well. I got asked about the recipe by a customer at lunch and when I told her it was a trade secret but suggested we might be putting the sauces in stock in the near future, I had a lot of good feedback."

"That's great to hear. So tell me your ideas."

Cora sipped her coffee and sighed. "This is good, thank you. Right, well Rob and I talked it over. If we bottle the sauce, we could have different heat levels. Rob said it won't be hard to do. And perhaps we could also add a chili jam. I know your mom makes it because I've tasted it. Do you think she'd be keen?"

"It was her idea in the first place. She keeps bringing it up and so far I've been too busy. You've seen her garden, right? It's got every chili known to man in it. Anything you want to try that's hot and spicy, she grows it."

"And we were thinking of other items people can use at home for their own barbeques. Rob's spicy batter, the one he uses on the onion rings for example. He gets asked what's in that all the time." She glanced at Duke and smiled. "Oh, to be in such demand."

"Now you see why the restaurant works so well. The food we produce is what people keep coming back for. It was Mama's sauces that got me into the restaurant in the first place. Did I tell you that?"

She tilted her head. "No, you didn't."

He put his mug on the coffee table and took her hand sending a delicious shiver up her spine. "Mama is at her best in the kitchen—always has been. Her Creole roots come across in her cooking and as a kid, I couldn't help but be involved with it. We all got roped in in some way with the kitchen chores. We grow the best beef in Texas on the ranch, at least in my opinion, and with her spices and sauces, I figured it was a perfect match. Adam, Dad and Grandpa have the ranch all but sorted and I tended to lean more toward the business side of things. I was helping Mama one day when she suggested I open a restaurant."

Cora grinned and Duke wound his fingers through hers. Rob hadn't told her it was Babs idea.

"I started to look around and decided a good rib and steak joint wouldn't go astray. Rob was the perfect choice for chef and we've known each other forever. We caught up one day not long after I was giving my own restaurant some thought and the rest, as they say, is history."

"A match made in heaven."

A light flickered in his eyes. "You could say that. It's been a hard few years but it's paying off now. The biggest thing for me is making sure that it continues to grow and I think Mama's sauces would help keep the momentum going. Kind of keep the restaurant front of people's minds when they're at home, know what I mean?"

"I do." She sipped her coffee. "You don't want to open another restaurant now you know you can do it?"

He laughed. "You don't think I have enough stress already?"

She shrugged.

"No. Not even interested. I'm happy with one restaurant because I want to make sure I can have a life myself, that I can consider my options."

Heat flushed her cheeks before she could stop it. Cora pulled her hand away and lifted her cup to her lips, hoping to cover her embarrassment.

Sure, she wanted to build her family too and it would be nice if it was with Duke or someone like him. But with her past and the baggage she still carried, finding someone as nice as Duke wasn't something she ever thought possible. Better to be happy with what she had now than risk heartache all over again.

"There're a couple of questions around the recipe and keeping the integrity of your mama's sauces a secret." She chewed on her lip for a second. "Rob is keen to the process happening. The profit margin will be better if we do it inhouse too."

"But he works too hard already. It's one reason we've never gotten past thinking about it."

Cora nodded. "I hear you but how about if we take on a first year chef to help him? Or even a second year. The thing is, I don't like having Rob as the only person in that kitchen who knows everything. If something happens to him, we're screwed."

"He'll be fine. Never had a day off sick, ever and the prep guys know how he does the meat, so it's not like he doesn't have back up. Guy has the constitution of a bull."

"That may be so but you hired me for a reason and

you're getting my advice. You probably thought you were bullet proof too and look what happened. How long since he's had a holiday?" She watched him over the rim of her coffee cup.

Duke scratched his chin and avoided looking in her eyes. "Not sure to be honest."

"He hasn't had one since you opened the restaurant. I checked. Look, he may be a good worker and your friend but as you know yourself, things happen. We can't afford to lose him, even for a few days with the flu. Sure, the kitchen staff could probably throw a steak and a rack of ribs on the grill. But if he goes down for more than a couple of days..."

"What does Rob think?"

"I told him that I refused to even think about him doing the sauces unless he takes on an apprentice. He scowled, pretty much like you're doing now. That changed once I reminded him of what happened to you for doing too much." She met his gaze. "One of the prep guys put his hand up to be his sidekick. The restaurant can more than afford it. What do you think?"

"You don't need my permission to hire staff, Cora. You're the manager and I trust you." Duke sucked in a breath. "I can imagine Rob when you gave him the ultimatum. You hit below the belt, you know that – right?"

Cora grinned. "I also know my job." She did. But what she didn't know was what to do with these feeling that kept pushing to the surface. How could she be falling for the man who was not only her boss, but who could singlehandedly ruin her life with the click of his fingers?

When Duke said goodnight, he stopped at the door.

"Cora, thanks for stepping up. You have no idea how much I appreciate it."

She leaned on the door frame, and gave a small yawn. Her bed had been calling for the last ten minutes but she was loath to push Duke out while they were so comfortable talking. "Same here, for looking out for Toby, I mean."

He lifted a finger and stroked it down her cheek.

She froze. Was she ready for this? Did she want him to kiss her goodnight? Cora swallowed trying to ignore the internal argument between her heart and her brain.

"He's a lovely kid and a credit to you. The whole family are besotted with Toby."

"Thanks. He's a good boy." A sigh escaped her lips and she leaned closer to him. "Duke?"

"Yes?"

"I...look, I think...."

He dropped a quick kiss on her forehead. "Stop thinking so hard, Cora and go to bed. You're probably beat." He winked at her, turned and walked away, his hands jammed in his jeans pockets, a spring in his step.

Was he flirting with her now? She touched her fingers to her skin where his lips had pressed and shut the door. There were so many reasons why she shouldn't get involved—but try telling that to her thudding heart.

CHAPTER THIRTEEN

D uke sat with his laptop at the kitchen island while his mama cooked. The silence of his bedroom drove him downstairs to search for someone to talk to.

"What are you doing, Duke?"

"Searching for Daniel and Lissa. There has to be some sign of them out there. Surely someone has seen them."

Mama folded the cloth in her hand and put it down before speaking. "Sugar, if Clay and that P.I. we hired can't find them, I don't think you're going to have much luck."

Duke scrawled through the pages as he spoke. "Never give up, Mama. You never know when you're going to find a little thread that will send you down the right track."

"What did you put in the search bar?" She moved around, stood beside him and glanced over his shoulder at the screen.

"Women on the run from the law with their kids."

"That's nasty, Duke. Some of these poor women probably have a good reason to run."

Some did, he agreed. But not his sister-in-law, Lissa. She'd lost that custody case.

"Holy shit." He stopped scowling and clicked on the headline. "That's Cora, I'm sure it is."

Babs leaned in for a closer look as he brought up the newspaper picture. "Oh my."

With his mom hovering over his shoulder, Duke read the news report. Cora had been arrested after causing bodily harm to her partner, leaving him lying in a pool of blood. There was a photo of Cora, her hands cuffed behind her back as the police bundled her into a waiting car. The blood on her shirt was obvious.

His mama put a hand on his back and rubbed it up and down as she read the story along with him.

"There has to be an explanation for what she did, Duke. Don't go blaming her before you know it all, now, you hear me?"

"It doesn't look good. But we've had experience with this. We know how things can get taken out of context. Look what Lissa did to Adam, the way she tried to tarnish his name when she lost the court case. And look at how many people believed it until the real truth came out." He finished the story and scrolled to another related news link. "Apparently she ran with Toby. This man claims she didn't have the authority to do that. Mama, she doesn't seem the type to do the wrong thing."

Mama bustled back around the other side of the island counter. "Exactly. So don't go playing judge and jury until the poor girl gets to say her piece. Don't want you barking up the wrong tree and ruining what you have with her."

"We don't have anything." Maybe that was a good thing if

he was to believe this news report. He followed another link in the story and cringed when he saw photos of a blood splattered knife and the wounds on her partners body.

"Don't you go lying to me, sugar. I've seen the way you look at Cora, like a bee eyeing off a field of cornflowers. Give the poor girl a chance to explain before you go crucifying her and dumping her into the same barrel as Lissa."

"She lied to me. Said he was living in another state and trouble to be around. Never once did she mention getting arrested for stabbing him. Neither, for that matter, did Bo. I trusted him."

"As I said, Duke, you need to hear her side of the story before you go jumping to conclusions. I don't believe she has a mean bone in her body to be honest and nor do you. If she stabbed someone, likely they deserved it."

"I liked her, Mama. Like, really liked her." He shut the laptop and wiped a hand over his face. Duke felt gutted, as if someone had tripped him up and left him lying on the pavement.

"So ask. What harm can that do?" His mother turned on the oven and adjusted the trays before sliding in the cakes she said she was cooking for morning tea. "She hasn't gone in yet. Go talk to her. Toby will probably be down with Grandpa and that little dog of his causing all kinds of fun. You're the boss and can make her late for work if you want to."

Cora was putting the finishing touches on the bed making before heading to the restaurant when there was a tap on the door. She walked out and saw Duke standing there, a frown on his face. After last night when he'd all but kissed her. How long would it be before she saw him again?

"Hey." She held the door open and caught him staring over the pasture.

He turned to her, his eyes cold sending shivers down her spine. What had she done to deserve that kind of look?

"We need to talk." He dug his hands in his jeans pockets.

"Come in."

Duke shook his head. "No thanks. What I have to say can be said out here unless you're scared of someone overhearing what the true Cora is like?"

Her belly rolled and she held her arms around herself. This wasn't sounding good at all. "I don't know what you mean." Cora licked her lips, her throat closing over in dread.

"You stabbed your boyfriend and stole your son according to a news report. At first I didn't believe it but when I saw you were arrested and charged, I started to question if I was being gullible believing everything you said. When were you going to tell me about that? In fact, when were you going to tell the family about what you've done? With what's happening with Adam, did you not think we had a right to know? Did you not think it would be something we *should* know?"

"It's none of your business."

"Bullshit! We're a little bit oversensitive when it comes to parents running with their child in case you hadn't noticed."

He shook his head as if he didn't believe her and stepped away before rounding on her again. "I gave you a job. Gave you a home. Heck, I even took you into my parents' house."

"And I appreciate it too."

He laughed, a bitter sound that dug into her, tearing at her hard won independence. "I bet you did. I never thought I'd be protecting someone who could do what you did."

The skin on the back of her neck prickled and Cora saw red. "What, protect my son from a violent person? Stand up for myself and fight for what I thought was right?" She sucked in a deep breath even though all she wanted to do was hide and cry in pain that the man she thought would be different, could be different, was in fact more of the same. She'd thought Duke was special. That he could be trusted and that he cared for her. He couldn't even ask what had happened. Instead he went straight for the kill and blamed her. Just like her ex had done when he'd been the one to stuff up their relationship.

"If he was the violent one, then how come the police arrested you for attempted murder? If he was so violent, why was he the one who ended up with a knife in his back? I wanted to believe the best of you, Cora. Even reading the newspaper reports I had a pang of conscience. Maybe they were wrong but then I remembered what you told me about him being in a different state. You actually lied to me. That's the hard part."

He'd been reading old newspaper reports on her! The ones that were more concerned with the flashy headlines and not the whole truth. Where had they been when the police found out the real story and dropped the charges? Where were they when she went for full custody and got it?

Oh, that's right. Not worthy headlines.

She'd really thought better of Duke. It hurt that she had to defend herself to him but what choice did she have? Cora loved her job, loved living here at the ranch and was loathe to drag her little boy away from people that obviously adored him.

She took a steadying breath. "Because if I hadn't done it, Toby would be dead now. Next time you see my son, take note of the scar down below his left ear. The one that runs under his chin and stops short of his jugular. His father did that to him. I stopped him the only way I could—by fighting back with the first thing I could grab. A kitchen knife."

Duke stared at her, mouth open.

"He wasn't even two years old so lucky for me he barely remembers it. So next time you decide to jump in and defend someone you don't know over something you had no knowledge over other than dated tabloid reports, stop and think for a moment. What would you do in my place if someone held a knife to your child's throat in an attempt to strip you of your savings so he could buy drugs?"

Duke paled and his throat worked but she wasn't finished. He'd started this, she would say what she wanted without him interrupting. "I'd do it all again. So if that makes me a bad person, so be it. Maybe I did lie to you. I should've told you he was in prison but I don't like the tarnish that leaves on me. Even though it's not my fault he's there. I'm sorry that my lie hurts you so much. But I will not stand by and let you or anyone else run me into the ground for doing what any good mother would do given the chance."

"He tried to hurt Toby?"

"If you bothered to dig a little deeper, you would've found out that minor detail. But you got sucked in by the headlines. I get that."

"No, I…"

"Now who's lying, Duke?" She shook her head and continued. "He got a good lawyer and had the charge downgraded from attempted murder to assault, spent nine months in jail for it but that will never be enough for us. The police apologized but that didn't take away the trauma they put me through. That man is a danger to my son and that's why I had to move despite the fact that the courts gave me full custody. He's doing another stint for assault and is due out shorty. I know how he works, he always comes looking for us to cause trouble. That part is true." She watched the anger replaced with doubt, realization and then sorrow mixed with a healthy dose of regret.

"I know you're only angry with me because of what happened to Adam but not all woman do the wrong thing by their husbands, Duke. Some of us have no other way to survive, to keep our children safe but to run. Please don't let that color what you think of us moms with no choice who do the right thing."

"I don't know what to say."

"Goodbye would suit me right now. I need to get ready for work." She stepped inside the door and slammed it shut in his face before breaking down into tears.

CHAPTER FOURTEEN

Cora didn't know how she got through the rest of the week. At work, she felt wooden, hollow and didn't know which way to go. Should she leave and find something else? Should she stay and try to ignore the pain she was in?

The thought wasn't inviting. She loved her new job, the tiny cottage she called home and Duke's family. Toby had never been so happy and if she decided to move, it would kill him. This was the first time her little boy had been around a normal family and to take that away from him would be mean and petty.

But the thought of being around Duke was killing her too. She'd had vague dreams in the beginning about the two of them getting together. Dreams that she'd tried to squash because of the circumstances. She'd failed and that was the reason she was hurting so much now.

Even if she understood why Duke said what he did, she didn't want to forgive him for jumping to conclusions without asking her first. To her, trust was everything.

Who in their right mind believed everything they found on the internet?

He'd tried to apologize, multiple times but Cora didn't want to know. She walked away whenever he tried and he finally got the message that he'd hurt her too much. She ignored his phone calls unless he called her at the office regarding work. She didn't know how she was going to cope now he was allowed back. Almost two weeks off and the doctor finally gave him the all clear to return. It played on her mind and she could feel herself getting more and more agitated.

Rob walked into her office the day before Duke announced he was coming back to work. He took a seat in front of her desk and waited for her to finish her phone call.

"Want to talk about it?"

She tucked a curl behind her ear and looked at her computer screen, keen to avoid eye contact. If Duke was calling in his friend to sort out his problems for him, he was going to be disappointed. She liked Rob but this wasn't his business. "No thanks."

"How about you listen then?" He leaned forward and rubbed his fingers together. "Duke called me and told me what he did to you. Wanted to make sure that you were okay."

Cora bit back a retort. It would do no good letting her bad mood out on Rob, even if he was Duke's best friend.

"Thing is, he was a dick. I told him so too, in case you're interested in my opinion. He let his emotions get to him and he knows it."

She spoke without looking at him. "People shouldn't believe everything they read on the internet. Sadly they do."

Rob nodded. "Yeah, they do. Unfortunately, Duke was having a bad day and he wasn't thinking straight. He blames himself for Lissa taking Daniel from Adam."

"What for?"

"Because he was responsible for introducing her to Adam. He knew she had a drug problem when she was younger and everyone thought she was clean. Otherwise he wouldn't have done it. Duke believes everyone deserves a second chance. She proved him wrong. Poor guy hasn't stopped blaming himself."

Cora picked up a ballpoint and clicked it a few times before throwing it down on her desk in frustration. "I understand all of that but it still pisses me off that he didn't ask me what happened. He assumed and that really gets on my nerves. Where was the trust, Rob?"

"He knows that now and believe me, he's sorry. I like you Cora and I don't want to see you go. I know you're thinking about it; I can see it in your eyes. Kind of figured with him coming back tomorrow, you'd be a bit anxious." He leaned forward and gave her a smile. "Care to tell me what really happened? I make a good listener apparently."

Cora blinked back the sudden emotion that welled up. It'd been so long since she'd had anyone to talk to. Robs offer was too good to turn down. He was a nice guy. Gentle, caring and kind to the staff that worked with him. She could use the friend. "Sure you want to hear all the sordid details?"

He leaned back and crossed one leg over the over, a smile crossing his face. "Go for it. I'm ahead of schedule anyway."

Cora gave him the watered down version of her life from the fateful meeting of Toby's father until now.

"You're one strong lady. I knew you were when I met you."

"Thanks. Don't actually feel like it some days." She pulled a tissue from her pocket, dabbed her eyes and sighed. "I should talk to Duke about this."

"Your call, Cora but I know he's hurting that he jumped to conclusions. His mama would've whopped his ass good, I can tell you that for nothing too."

She burst out laughing at the image that came to her mind.

Rob grinned. "True story. She would. Babs loves that little man of yours. When she dropped those chilies off to me the other week, all she could talk about was Toby. She misses young Daniel like crazy."

"It would be hard, I get that." She chewed on her bottom lip. "Maybe I've tortured him long enough."

"Maybe. Maybe not. That's a decision I'm happy to leave to you. So long as you know you have my support, go for gold. Won't hurt Duke to wallow a bit in his own stupidity. Might make him think a bit before he opens that mouth of his." He stood, stretched his back. "Right, I'd better go check on the kitchen." He walked to the door and paused. "Listen, those recipes of Babs. I'm glad you decided to keep it in house too, and if you insist on promoting Chris to help me, so be it. He'll make a good apprentice and he's pretty keen to learn. But I'm happy to see if I can manage making small batches before we go employing anyone else to take his place. It's not like it's going to take a heck of a lot of time out of my day. The rest of the kitchen team can prep some of it and it'll simmer away along with the ribs and everything else that has to cook slow." He scratched his chin.

"Works for me."

Rob slapped his hand against the door frame and grinned. "Good. It's not like we need to make huge batches at once. Just enough to sell at the front desk."

"I guess that could work. I'll hunt out a graphic artist and see what we come up with."

He nodded. "Let me know when you're ready with it and I'll get a hold of Babs. She can help with the first batch. It'll make her proud and she's probably the only woman I don't mind sharing a kitchen with. She's like a second mom to me."

"So long as you're sure the kitchen will still run smoothly. I don't want to overwork anyone."

He laughed. "Not going to happen. I take good care of myself and I'm not one to stress like Duke is. Besides, with Chris stepping up a notch, the rest of the kitchen staff are all happy to help and grab a few more hours. They know what I do and can take over in a pinch, and just to make you happy, I'll take care to teach them more of what I do. Catch you later." He slapped his hand on the door frame again and left her chewing over her options.

She could accept Duke's apology and move on. But would she ever be able to forgive him for doubting her just when she was beginning to think she should give him a chance? Would it dig at her every time something happened that he didn't trust her enough to ask for the truth?

Duke waited for ten minutes after he heard Cora drive past the main house before he went outside. The lights were on in the cottage and he could see her through the window. He wiped his palm over his jeans and gave himself a verbal telling off. No matter how many times he went over it, he couldn't get past the fact that he'd been so stupid and so wrong.

Cora was the best thing that had happened to this family in ages and Mama was justifiably worried he'd scared her off. She was waiting for the resignation letter to hit the kitchen counter. He couldn't let that happen and not just because he was worried his mom would kick his ass either.

Tomorrow he was allowed back at work and he didn't want to run into any issues. If she was going to tear a strip off of him, he'd rather she do it now away from the restaurant. He was prepared for the worst but was hoping for the best. Not that he thought he deserved it.

By the time he'd walked down to the cottage, Duke'd broken out into a nervous sweat. What if she sent him away? He wanted more from her than just a restaurant manager. He wanted a relationship with this strong, feisty woman. Someone beside him who was prepared to go through hell and back for her family. Someone who didn't let negative attitudes and events stop her from raising her son alone. A son that the whole family had fallen in love with.

He'd read a story to Toby as he fell asleep tonight. Duke had watched the way the boys lashes had shadowed his cheeks as he fell asleep, how Toby's hand had been on Duke's arm from beginning to end. How at ease he'd felt with the child, as if it was the most natural thing in the world to drop a kiss goodnight on his forehead as he closed the book.

Now he had to convince his mother of how much he regretted his earlier actions and try to make her stay.

The door opened and Cora stared at him. "Duke. What are you doing here? Is Toby okay?" She looked past him into the night.

"He's fast asleep and fine. This isn't about Toby, Cora. It's about me and you. You won't take my calls unless its business so I figured I should come down and clear the air before I start back tomorrow." He held out the posy of Texas Bluebonnets he'd picked earlier when he wandered the pasture with Toby and his pup. Something about the color reminded him of Cora's eyes. "I picked you these today. Toby said they're your favorite color."

A smile twitched the corners of her lips and he silently thanked Toby for telling him. "He did, huh?"

"Yeah."

She moved back and held the door open, closing it behind him when he passed her.

Duke turned to face her, ready to apologize.

Cora held up her hand. "Stop." She walked into the kitchen and took a mason jar from the shelf, filled it with water and placed the flowers in it. "Have a seat." She leaned on the kitchen counter while Duke sat on the couch.

"I'm sorry for ignoring you but you pissed me off, big time."

Duke opened his mouth but she stopped him again.

"Wait, okay. Let me say this first and then the floor is all yours." She folded her arms and glanced down at her feet a moment before looking him in the eye. "You were kind of right, in a way. I did run with Toby when I shouldn't have. But it's nothing like your sister-in-law. Unlike her, I got full custody from the courts. But what I didn't mention was that John is supposed to have contact with him every month."

"But he's in jail again. How is that fair on you?"

She gave him a smile that turned into a frown. "That's the thing. In my eyes the courts let me down more than I've let John down by running. His attack on Toby was horrific and they got it downgraded because I stabbed him. John's lawyer said I caused the attack on Toby, that if I'd walked away it never would've happened. I could have prevented it if I'd only called the police. They said it was all my fault."

"But he tried to kill his own son." Duke couldn't believe what he was hearing.

"I know but lawyers are good at twisting words. The judge didn't wholly agree but at the same time he had more sympathy for John than he deserved. His lawyer was good."

"Why did you come here then, Cora?"

"Because when he gets out of jail, he'll come for us. He did last time after he got out and the cops couldn't do anything about it because he had visitation rights. Mind you, they had to be supervised visits and so far he's refused to take advantage of that. I somehow doubt that he's changed much during this latest stint in jail. As far as I'm concerned, he can't be trusted not to hurt Toby and I won't give him that chance. I know him better than the courts do. He has a vindictive streak a mile wide. Nobody gets the better of him, ever."

"How many times has he been inside? You said he went

in for assault but I'm not sure if you meant the assault on you and Toby or someone else."

She took a breath. "John originally got put away for drugs charges. I testified against him. When he got out, he attacked Toby because I wouldn't give him money. Claimed I owed him." She shrugged. "Then he assaulted someone when he was released for that and got another stint behind bars. He's due out any time now. I wasn't prepared to wait for him to come out again nor did I have the time or the money to go back to court and ask for the contact to be limited if at all. I knew that the next time I saw him he'd be more dangerous."

"And I treated you like crap over it." He stood up. "I'm so very sorry, Cora. I can't believe I did that to you and you're still here. Mama was sure you'd hand me your notice." He grimaced.

She laughed and shook her head. "I'm not that much of a snowflake. I did consider it for all of two days." Imagine if she'd taken off as was her first impulse. She would've lost so much. The time for running away was over. She felt safe here, and Toby was the happiest he'd ever been.

"I love my job, my home and your family. Sure, you pissed me off to start with but I understand because of what your family has gone through. I'm disappointed in you for not asking me before you judged me though. It took a couple of days for me to forgive you."

He sucked in a breath and stepped closer, reaching for her. "You forgive me?"

"In the scheme of things, it wasn't the worst thing that's happened in my life, so yeah, I forgive you. This time."

She didn't protest when he pulled her into his arms and

held her against his chest. It could easily have gone the other way but someone was looking out for him, he was sure of it. Duke cupped the back of her head and looked into her eyes. "I don't deserve you, you know that?"

Her lips curved into a genuine smile. "Maybe. We all make mistakes, I get that but I want this to be the last one between us. I'm not interested in fighting all the time, Duke. Not with my boss or my boyfriend if this is where it's going. I want an easy life—no drama. Can you do that?"

"I can do whatever you want so long as you give me a chance." He dipped his head and touched his lips to hers. Slowly at first, he tasted and teased. When she responded and leaned into his chest, he put his arms around her and teased her tongue with his. He'd come so close to pushing her away. What a fool!

He nibbled at her bottom lip, his heart racing but in a good way. Her small moan of pleasure thrilled him. Duke paused for a breath, relieved Cora had forgiven him and was open to continuing their friendship. He wouldn't have coped if she'd refused to talk to him.

Dark shadows clung under her eyes and he felt a moment of remorse. She was tired and needed sleep. "Listen, I should go and let you get some rest. Tomorrow will come around way too soon."

She yawned and covered her mouth with her hand. "I'm pretty beat. I feel better now we've spoken though."

Duke kissed the tip of her nose. "Me too. I'll leave you alone, as much as I hate the idea, and see you for breakfast in the morning?"

Cora nodded. "Sure."

He left her alone and headed back to the big house, his

heart much lighter than it had been for days. The dark cloud that had been dogging him the last couple of days had gone, leaving behind clear skies, filled with possibilities. Cora cared about him. She was going to stay. That alone was going to let him sleep well tonight.

CHAPTER FIFTEEN

"Eli, can you suggest someone to fix this?" Duke called his brother early the next morning and told him Cora's story, hopeful that he could help her in some way. "She needs to be able to protect herself and Toby."

His brother sighed over the phone. "Dude, you woke me up for a recommendation for another lawyer?"

Duke rolled his eyes. He'd forgotten what crazy hours Eli kept. "Of course I did—and your advice. Plus I don't want to start this if there's no chance of Cora getting what she needs. She's been through enough. If you were here, I'd make an appointment and ask you in person but since you can't pull yourself away from your elite athletes, I have to ask advice only over the phone."

Eli rattled off a couple of names and Duke wrote them down. Then he gave his learned opinion about Cora's chances of getting the visitation order stopped. Any man that tried to kill his own child didn't deserve to have that right as far as Duke was concerned. His brother agreed. "Thanks. Listen, when are you coming home for a visit?"

"Might be sooner than you think. I need a break, man. This job is killing me."

Words he never thought he'd hear from his little brother. "I know the feeling." He told Eli what had happened to him along with words of wisdom. "You don't want to go there, bro. It's unpleasant and you can imagine what Mama was like."

There was a pang of longing in Eli's voice. "I miss her. I miss all of you."

This was the first time his brother had admitted he wanted out of the fast lane and it tore at Duke's heart. "Come home, Eli. Start a law practice here. Life's too short to burn out over prima donna stars. You've given them enough of your good years. Think of yourself for a change."

"I'm tossing it over, believe me but don't you dare tell the folks until I say so. Got it?"

"Yeah, bro. I got it. Thanks and talk soon, okay? Keep me informed about what you're doing." He was on a high with the thought of his brother coming home. "I can't wait to see you again. It's been too damn long since we shared a beer and talked about nothing in particular together." They could sit for hours soaking up the peace and Duke missed that.

"Sure." Eli hung up and Duke started making calls. An hour later, he walked into Cora's office but she wasn't there. He headed down to the kitchen and found her talking to Rob.

"Hey, guys. I spoke to Eli and I have news, Cora. Want to do this in the office?"

She shook her head. "No, Rob knows about John. It's okay."

He shared a smile with his best friend. "Right. I spoke to Eli this morning about you going back to court and asking to have the visitation order changed or stopped considering your ex's history of not having any contact with Toby. With his stint in jail, he doesn't seem to think it will be hard to do. Especially since it was you who called the police every time he got nasty and it's all on record."

Her face lit up. "Really? That would be amazing. We have nobody there for support like we do here. I don't want to go back if John's not even going to bother." She bit her lip. "Did he say how much he thinks it will cost? I have a small savings now thanks to your dad not taking much for rent but I can't afford a high-priced lawyer."

"It should only take one court date according to Eli because everything is on record. You belong here and so does Toby." He grinned at Rob and changed the subject before she got hung up on the cost, which he was prepared to pay himself just to ease her mind. "Mama is getting excited about the products going on sale. What have you decided between you?"

Rob wiped his hands on his apron and told him their plans. "Cora has organized a graphic artist to do the labels." He stepped over to the notice board and pulled down a sheet of paper. "Here are a couple of early ideas. What do you think?"

Duke looked at them. "Nice. I really like the first one— very New Orleans like. Mama would be impressed."

"That's what we figured. I'm waiting for a final proof before I bring it home and show your parents."

"She's going to love it." Duke pegged the sheet back up. "Are you sure you're up to speed with this production idea?"

Rob nodded his head to the storeroom. "Sure are. We got bottles delivered the other day. So long as you don't go selling it in bulk to anyone, we should be fine."

Duke shook his head. "Not going to happen. The only place it will be on sale is in this restaurant, that I can promise you, and only to customers. No bulk deals so another restaurant can use it. That was the only stipulation that Mama had. And that she could come in and help when she felt like it."

Rob grinned. "I figured that already. I have no problems with her being here. She's a breath of fresh air."

"Man, you need to get out more. Don't you remember back in school when we couldn't wait to get out of her sight?"

Rob sighed and shook his head, sharing a quick glance with Cora. "That was you, Duke. Not me. I loved hanging out in the kitchen with her. If it wasn't for your mama, I doubt I would've taken up this career."

Cora laughed. "Looks like you're outnumbered, Duke. We both think your mama is amazing."

"Maybe it's time you moved out of home, man." Rob picked up his tongs and turned over a set of ribs. "You're old enough to be more independent, don't you think?"

He glanced at Cora who looked away, a hint of pink on her cheeks. What on earth was Rob thinking, saying that in front of her? Sure they'd just potentially started something but he didn't want to rush her into a relationship. He wanted to move slow and steady. Duke didn't want her to think she was being pushed.

"Nah, not yet. All the other kids have left home and she hates not having them around. If I moved out, she'd never forgive me. One day I will but not yet." He rubbed his hands together. "I have things to do, talk to you two later." Duke turned and headed back to his office.

"That was interesting." Rob dropped the hood on his grill and turned to Cora.

"Why?"

"Well, I figured Duke would want to have more space to himself now you two've sorted out your problems. You have, haven't you?"

Cora looked down at her feet. "Yes, we have. He apologized and I forgave him."

Rob roared with laughter. "Oh Babs is gonna love that. Him staying home will have her planning your wedding before you know it. Mark my words."

Cora sighed. "Not if I can help it. I'm not ready for anything like that. I have my son to think about and a career I want to work at." She turned away so Rob wouldn't see the blush that had no doubt swept over her cheeks. It might be bad timing or circumstance but Cora was open to a relationship with Duke but only if the stars aligned and things worked out the way she wanted them to. No chance was she going to get involved if he couldn't remain calm and supportive. Nor if her ex started causing problems because that would make things very uncomfortable for everyone.

She smiled as she drove into the ranch later that afternoon. It would be the first time in weeks that she'd gotten home before dark since Duke had been taken ill. Even her days off had been put on hold. Not that she minded working hard while Duke was out of action; she was used to it. But she'd missed having dinner with her boy, the fun of bath time and putting Toby to sleep at night, their bedtime stories and snuggling with her little man.

She parked at the cottage and got out, glancing around hoping to see her son. There was plenty of movement on the ranch but none of it seemed to feature Toby. Foals in the pasture beside her cottage frolicked in the long grass and a patient mare stood watch over them. Down at the barn, the sound of cattle rumbled through the air and a tractor chugged past the cottage, the cowboy raising a hand in greeting.

She opened the door and moved inside, dumping her bag as she went. She wanted a change of clothes and then a walk around to find him and to breathe in the clean country air.

Cora was doing up the button on a pair of worn jeans when she heard footsteps outside and a knock on her door. "Cora, you in there?"

"Coming." She brushed her hand over her hair as she walked out. "Hey, Babs, everything okay?"

Duke's mom smiled. "Of course it is. I heard you drive past and wanted to bring down dinner for you. Last thing you want to do on your first night off is to cook. Taking the slack for Duke was such a big job and we appreciate it, sugar." She bustled into the kitchen and placed the covered dish on the counter. "You want to spend the time with that little man of yours, not in the kitchen."

"You're very sweet, thank you so much." Cora walked

over and reached for Babs but the woman was ahead of her. She grabbed Cora in a big hug and held her tight.

"I'm overbearing and annoying, I get that. My boys tell me all the time I go overboard but I can't help it. I like to smother those I love with my brand of kindness and that includes my cooking."

Cora breathed in her scent. A mix of floral perfume and spices from her cooking. She missed having family like this around and was grateful for Babs and everything she did.

"I don't find you overbearing, Babs, not at all. You've done more for Toby and me than anyone else has ever done. I don't know how to thank you." She held Bab's hands, squeezing them gently. "We really appreciate what you've done. Welcomed us into your family, given us this home and practically taken over raising my son for me while I worked. You're an angel."

Babs smiled and her eyes filled with tears. As she sniffed, she wiped her eyes. "Of course I helped. What person wouldn't? You've given us so much by taking over the business while Duke recovered. If it wasn't for you, I doubt he would've taken off any time at all, let alone almost two weeks." She sniffed. "If it wasn't for you, I never would've had so much time with my boy. It's me who is thankful, Cora."

Cora wrapped her arms around Babs shoulders. "Well, let's just agree that we appreciate each other then. And thank you for dinner. I hadn't even given cooking a thought to be honest. I was more interested in finding my child and spending time with him."

"He's down in the barn with Grandpa. He's so in love with that calf that lost its mama, and bottle feeding it is his job. Toby can't seem to leave it alone. I reckon he'd sleep with it given half a chance."

The idea didn't surprise her. Her little man had always been an animal person. They'd never had the opportunity to own a pet before and that was why Grandpa had brought in the puppy. She'd always been working and their landlord hadn't been a fan of animals in his properties. "I'll go and drag him away. I need me some loving from that little boy."

Babs walked with her to the door. "You and Duke. I hope I'm not putting my nose where it's not wanted and my son's love life is not my business, Cora, but I wanted to let you know that you'd be very welcome in this family if that's the way it turned out. We're all in love with the pair of you already."

Duke would have a fit if he could hear his mom talking. He had warned her though so Cora ran with it. "I'm not sure that will happen Babs but thank you. Regardless of whether something develops or not, we couldn't have ended up at a better place." She closed the door and gave Babs one more hug. "Now, let me find my son before I bust." *And you start talking babies too.*

CHAPTER SIXTEEN

Cora leaned over the fence and met Grandpa's gaze as he stood behind her little boy. Toby held the bottle to the calf's mouth, struggling to hold onto it. The brown and white calf was down on its front legs, its head tilted up and milk bubbles dribbled from its mouth. The hungry baby guzzled from the bottle, nudging it every few sucks to bring down the milk as it would've if it was nursing from its mama. Each nudge sent her little boy back a few paces but Grandpa was there to prop him up if needed.

"That's one hungry baby. You're doing a fine job, Toby."

Toby glanced up at her and smiled just as the calf nudged the bottle again.

A shadow moved beside her and Adam leaned over the fence. "Doing a great job, Toby. Reckon you could take on another one?"

Toby's mouth dropped open. "Another one?" He glanced at Cora before nodding vigorously, distracted by the question. "Yes, sir." The calf sucked the last of the milk and nudged the bottle so hard it flipped it out of Toby's hands. He stumbled. Grandpa grabbed him and lifted him in the air.

"Wow, little cowboy. That steer is getting out of control. Better go see what Adam has for you." He handed Toby over the fence to Cora who grabbed him and held him tight.

"Missed you, Toby."

He flung his arms around her neck and squeezed tight. "Missed you too, Mom but you have to work. Same as me." He planted a wet kiss on her cheek and slid down, grabbing Adam's hand. He leaned down and patted his sleeping pup, snuggled up on an old sack outside the pen. "Us cowboys have more to do. Look after Lilly pup for me till I get back, okay?"

"Sure thing." She leaned down and picked up the tiny dog he'd named Lilly, holding it to her chest. It licked her fingers and settled against her.

Adam smiled and walked away with her son. She watched them go, her heart thumping with love for him and the way he'd come out of his shell since they'd been at the ranch.

"You have an amazing little fella there, Cora." Grandpa came out of the pen and stood beside her. "He's so keen to learn to be a cowboy. Reckon when it's time to go to school, you're going to have problems getting him on that bus."

"I certainly hope not but we'll sort that out when the time comes. I can't thank you enough for looking out for him. You have no idea how much I appreciate it." Toby and Adam walked out of sight into the other end of the barn.

"I reckon the feeling is mutual. That little man has touched more than this old man's heart. Adam is actually starting to smile again. Never thought I'd see the day, to tell you the truth."

"Duke told me. It's so sad he doesn't get to see his own son." She tried not to let the guilt of those words get to her. But her ex was different. He'd never wanted Toby.

"Yeah, it is but I have faith that one day we'll get Daniel back. He's always in our prayers."

"Duke feels terribly guilty about it too." The tiny pup whimpered in her arms and she glanced at it. It's little front paws twitched as it dreamed. Cora stroked a finger over its head and down its back to soothe it.

"Boy has no need to feel guilty. We all got taken in with her charms. Don't matter none now, as we got Daniel out of that volatile relationship. We'll get him back, just you wait and see."

"I hope so."

Toby strode back toward them, followed by Adam with a wriggling bundle of black and white in his arms.

"Looks like we're going to have a busy season." Grandpa scratched his prickly face. "Best we set up another stall for this calf too. Don't you go worrying about Toby. I'll drop him off on my way up to the big house later on at dinner time if that's okay?"

"Thanks, Grandpa. I'll take the pup and leave you cowboys to it."

"It's a big 'un, Mom." Toby stopped in front of her and tipped his head toward Adam. "Reckon he's gonna need a big bottle of milk to settle him down."

Cora glanced over his head at Adam who paused behind Toby with a smile on his face that bordered on sadness.

"I reckon you're right, little cowboy. This guy is going to

be a prize bull one day so you'd better take special care of him." He walked into the barn behind Grandpa and Toby and Cora left them to it.

Nothing she could do here—her son had everything under control. It might be time for a leisurely soak in the tub. She hadn't had one of those for so long, she'd forgotten just how good they were. Cora headed back to her cottage and placed the sleeping puppy in the dog bed in the corner of the lounge room. She filled the tub and lit a couple of scented candles in the bathroom. Cora drew the blinds and stripped off before climbing into the warm water.

As she lay back, she sighed in pleasure. This was perfect. Her son was happy, her job was secure and she was amongst good people. What more could a girl ask for? She closed her eyes and relaxed for the first time in weeks.

The move had been stressful but not as stressful as seeing Duke in pain and rushing him to the hospital. Now he was better and his health under control, she could stop worrying about him and start thinking about him in other ways. Was it a good idea to have a relationship with her boss? Considering she lived on the family ranch, would that be the wisest thing to do? What if it didn't work out? Would they still let her live here? Would Duke let her stay in her job or was she risking everything by falling for him?

Then there was Toby. Duke was a very different man to his father, but could she risk him feeling hurt or abandoned again? And would Duke even want a ready-made family?

She didn't know. All Cora knew was that now, for the first time in ages, she was comfortable, happy and the tension that usually sat between her shoulder blades was gone. Even with her ex due out of prison any day now, she didn't have the anxious feeling she usually did.

With Duke and his family behind her, Cora could deal with anything. Even John demanding his visitation rights, which she couldn't see happening in a million years.

D uke locked up the restaurant and smiled to himself. It was good to be back at work. Not that he minded being at home but it made him antsy to be doing nothing, especially when Cora was taking so much on her shoulders. She was great at her job, he knew that. But still, it made him feel guilty to throw so much her way when she was relatively new to the company.

She'd managed admirably in his absence too. The books were done, the staff happy and things were moving along with the in house production of his mom's sauces. They would be a good addition to the usual front of house sales like t-shirts and stickers. People always commented on them so it made sense. It also gave his mom something to be proud of.

He drove toward home, hoping like crazy that Cora's light was still on. He didn't want to be a pest but it would be nice to sit and talk about the day with her before he went to sleep. Then Duke started to feel guilty. It was her first early day and he didn't want to burden her with work but it was the only excuse he could think of for invading her space.

Man up, Duke and stop using work as an excuse. You've already kissed her once. She knew he wanted to have a relationship. He'd just cruise on past her place and see if he could get a cup of coffee before she went to bed. How hard could it be?

He held his breath as he turned into the driveway. Lights flickering in a couple of the cottages and the bunkhouse as he parked his truck in front of the big house. Cora was still awake. He wiped his palms on his jeans and took a couple of deep breaths. Then he strode past the house toward the cottage.

She answered on the first knock, almost as if she was waiting by the door. "Duke, hey."

"Cora. Hope I'm not disturbing you." His heart pounded in his ears.

She leaned on the door, a soft smile on her face. "No. I was just thinking about you, wondering if you'd closed up yet and how the day went."

He shrugged. "Yeah, it was good. No problems, everything is fine. I, ah, I just wanted to see you. To say goodnight and maybe have a quick chat if you don't mind." He gave a quiet laugh. "Seems I can't go to sleep without seeing your smile."

"You have some pretty words, Duke."

"I mean them. I know this," he indicated between them with his hand, "is still new but you mean a lot to me."

She smiled and held the door open. "Coffee?"

"Yeah, thanks." Duke followed her in as she shut the door. He wandered over to the kitchen and leaned on the counter while she filled the coffee machine. "How's Toby?"

"Great. I thought I'd get to spend an afternoon with him but he had other ideas. Not that I mind." She grinned and tucked a strand of hair behind her ear. "Adam found another calf that needed bottle feeding and Toby is in his element. That child was born to be a rancher."

"That's good. I'm pretty sure the family are all in agreement too. It's like he belongs here already." He reached out and stroked a finger down her cheek, feeling the shudder roll through her body. "You belong here too, Cora. I hope you know that."

"I feel more comfortable here than anywhere, to be honest. It's like I've come home. I never expected that." She reached for a coffee mug and poured Duke a drink before sliding it over the counter to him.

"Me either but I'm happy to go with it. Sometimes the most exciting things in life are the unexpected." He toyed with the handle on the mug. "I never expected to fall for you but I can't seem to help myself."

Her eyes widened and her mouth dropped open. Duke took the opportunity to lean over and place his lips on hers. Cora closed her eyes and a soft moan rose in her throat. Duke reached out and wound his hand behind her head, keeping her close so he could taste her, lose himself in the kiss.

She leaned into him, her arm going around his waist. Cora pressed against his chest and deepened the kiss.

She smelled of gardenia and sunshine. He slid his fingers through the silkiness of her hair, letting it fall through his fingers before cupping the back of her head. He didn't want to let her go.

"Mom." The frightened voice came from the doorway of the bedroom.

Cora froze in his arms.

"Let me." Duke pulled away, turned to Toby with a smile

on his face. "Hey, Toby. Or should I call you cowboy?" He reached out to her, stroking a hand up her arm to reassure her. Cora relaxed a little watching him. He smiled and turned back to her son.

Toby padded over to him, rubbing his eyes, his puppy following close by. When he stopped in front of Duke, the puppy plopped itself down by his feet. "I had a bad dream." His bottom lip wobbled as he stared at Duke.

Duke crouched down, reached out and pulled him to his chest. "Want to talk about it?"

Toby shook his head. "No."

"Okay then. How about we go sit on the couch until you feel better?" He smoothed his hand over Toby's back as the little boy leaned into his chest and walked him over to sit.

Cora moved around and took a chair not far from them, a sadness radiating from her that hit him in the gut. He winked, gave her a smile and continued to hold her son until Toby relaxed against him with a sigh.

"Ready for bed now, buddy?" Duke kept a hand on his shoulder.

"Yeah. I gotta get up early and feed the calves for Adam. We have lots of stuff going on." He slid from the couch and slapped his hand against his leg for the pup to follow as he padded back to bed.

Duke followed and waited until he'd climbed into bed and tucked the blankets under his chin. "If you need me, just call out, okay? I'll be sitting in the loungeroom talking to your mom."

Toby screwed up his face. "Are you going to be my dad, Duke? I don't have one and every kid needs a dad, right?"

"I don't know, Toby but I'll always be your friend. You can count on that one." He stroked Toby's hair from his face.

"And Grandpa, and Adam. I have lots of friends here. I'm a very lucky kid, aren't I?"

"You certainly are but so are we for getting to know you. Now close those eyes and go to sleep. You have a big day tomorrow."

"I sure do. After I feed the calves, Adam and Grandpa said I can go to town with them to the stock barn. We need more milk for the calves 'cause they're drinking so much!" He held his arms wide.

"Sounds like a good plan. Night now, Toby." Duke smiled at him and Toby's lashes settle on his cheeks as his eyes fluttered closed. Within seconds, he was asleep. Duke walked out, grabbing Cora's hand at the door where she stood watching.

"Thank you." Her eyes misted over.

"What for?"

"For being so kind to my son. Not everyone has that knack, especially his father."

"I didn't want to push in where I wasn't wanted but he came to me so I did what felt natural. He's a very cute kid and quite a character."

"He is although sometimes he can be a bit intense."

"Nah, he's a little kid who we've all fallen in love with. Talking of which, I'm pretty sure I was saying something along those lines before we were interrupted."

Cora grinned. "I believe you were."

He pulled her over to the couch after a final glance at Toby's door. When they were seated he slid his arm around her waist, leaned into her, and kissed her ear. "I can't help my feelings for you, Cora. I'm falling for you."

She shivered and a thrill shot through him. At least she wasn't immune to his charms. Lucky.

Cora turned her face to his, a small smile lifting the corners of her lips. "You are, huh?"

"I am. I hope you don't mind."

The tip of her tongue poked out and ran across the curve in her lips, sending a jolt down to his gut. "I'm starting to get to like the idea although I still have reservations, Duke."

"Do you mind if I try to convince you those reservations are unfounded?"

Cora tilted her head and smiled. "Okay."

Duke moved closer and kissed her softly at first. He savored the taste of her lips, the smell of her skin and the warm body that leaned into him farther. The hand that slid around his neck and the faint waft of perfume that reminded him of fresh flowers in the meadow on a summers day.

Her lips parted and Duke toyed with her tongue, gentle and seductive like a slow waltz. Braver now, he pressed her back against the couch, his hand slipping down her spine to rest in the curve of her back.

Cora pulled away, sucking in a deep breath. "Wow, that was some kiss, Duke." She fanned a hand in front of her face, the color high on her cheeks. "I haven't been kissed like that in years."

This was only the beginning as far as he was concerned. "Likewise. But I think it's wise that we leave it there or I won't be responsible for what happens next." He stood up, held his hand out to her.

Cora gripped his fingers and stood up, a smile lighting her eyes. "Thanks once again for being so good to my little man. I really appreciate it, Duke."

"There's no need to thank me. I'm already putty in his hands." He gave her a chaste peck on the cheek. "And Cora?"

"Yes?" she asked, the stars shining in her eyes.

"That's pretty much how I feel around you."

CHAPTER SEVENTEEN

The following day Cora sat at her desk looking at options for the labels for the in-house sauces when Duke burst into her office.

"Duke, have a look at these." Even as she said the words, a sense of dread shivered down her back. She stood and he reached for her. "What's going on?"

"I don't want you to panic yet but somethings happened." He tried to hold her against his chest but she pushed back.

"What is it? Is it Toby? Tell me what's going on."

"Adam just called. He's on his way to the hospital with Grandpa."

Her stomach dropped. "What happened?"

"They were at the stock feed place and Adam was at the back dock helping the staff load up the truck with calf milk and feed. Grandpa and Toby were looking at other things, not sure what. Doesn't really matter." A bead a sweat broke out on his top lip and she stared at it, willing herself not to lose control.

"Adam heard a cry and ran around the building.

Grandpa was on the ground, his leg at a strange angle. Toby was nowhere in sight."

Stars blurred her vision and a loud hum filled her ears. Cora swayed even though Duke held her. Her little boy was gone?

It didn't make sense. Until it did.

"And there's no chance he ran away scared?" Even as she asked the question, she knew the answer. "No it was John. His father has him." She pulled away and grabbed her purse and car keys. "I'm going into town. That bastard is not getting away with my son. He's done enough harm to last us a lifetime."

"I'll take you wherever you want to go but we're heading to the hospital first. There's nobody at the feed barn. Clay has his men out looking for your son. Don't you worry; he'll find him. My brother is a good man, Cora. He won't let anything happen to Toby."

"I'm going to take my car. I need to find my child. You don't know my ex. He'll do anything to get back at me for everything that's happened. He's a nasty vindictive person." She strode out of the office and Duke ran to keep up with her.

When they got to the parking lot, he guided her to his truck and it was only once she was in the seat that the trembling started. Her hands shook and she had to clamp her teeth together to still the tremble in her jaw. She couldn't let anything happen to her son. Not after everything they'd been through. She would find him. *Don't worry, baby. I'm coming for you. Nobody is going to keep us apart. I promise.*

They pulled up at the hospital and Cora jumped out of the truck before Duke turned it off. "Wait up." He grabbed her arm and walked her toward the emergency room where the ambulance would've taken Grandpa.

They found Adam pacing outside in the waiting room, his cell phone to his ear. When he saw Cora his face paled and he hung up.

"I'm so sorry, Cora. We'll find him, I promise. I just had to see to Grandpa first."

"I understand, Adam."

"Clay's all over it. I called him before the ambulance, Grandpa insisted on it."

Cora's eyes filled with tears but she lifted her chin and swallowed the sobs back. "How is he doing?"

Adam shrugged. "Don't know. They think his leg is broken but that's all I've been told. They're worried about his blood pressure because they might have to go in and pin it but he's a stubborn old coot. He's more worried about Toby."

"What happened, did he say?"

Adam took off his Stetson and wiped a hand over his short dark hair. "Yeah, according to Grandpa they'd wandered outside and were hunting for butterflies. Toby's fascinated with them and Grandpa is only too happy to oblige. Someone came up and started abusing him and next thing he knew, Grandpa was on the ground, his leg twisted underneath him. When he managed to take a breath and look around, Toby was being dragged into a car."

"What did the man look like?" Cora found his fingers and squeezed as she asked the question.

"Medium height, slim build, short cropped hair and a scar down his cheek. Pasty as well as if he hadn't been in the sun for a bit. You're thinking your ex, right?" Even as he said the words, Adam paled more. The significance wasn't lost on Duke. This wasn't going to happen to their family again. He wouldn't let it.

"Yeah. Sounds just like him." She finished speaking on a sob and Duke pulled her close.

"Hush now, Cora. We'll find him, I promise." Even as he said it, he shared a glance with his brother who shook his head. How could anyone believe his words when they hadn't been true before?

A door burst open and his parents hurried in. "Where is he? Someone tell me please before I lose my mind." His mom stared at him, her eyes filling, holding her hand over her heart.

"He's in the emergency room being checked out, still feisty as all heck so don't worry too much yet. If Grandpa is strong enough to insist on me calling Clay before the ambulance, he's going to be okay." Adam pulled her into a hug. "Mama, Toby is missing. Someone attacked Grandpa and took the little guy."

"No. Not that sweet little boy." She glanced at Cora. "Oh, you poor thing. What are we going to do?"

"Pretty sure Clay is all over it." His dad tried to calm her, patting her shoulder while Adam held her against his chest.

"He is." Adam swallowed and cleared his throat. "We called him as soon as I found Grandad and he has a team out searching. Whoever took Toby won't get far. Only one way out of town and that's got a roadblock on it already."

Bab's reached for Cora and folded her into her arms. "We'll find him, sugar. Don't you worry about that."

"What else is Clay doing?" his father asked.

"It'll no doubt be all over the local radio station by now. Clay would've called them to broadcast it. Anyone with a lick of sense would give up while he was ahead. If it was a local, they would know better. If it's Toby's father, he won't get far. The whole of Wishbone will be out there looking for him. You know how the good folk round here band together in times of crisis."

Babs smoothed down Cora's hair and wiped the tears from her cheeks. "Hear that, Cora? This town looks after its own and you and Toby are some of ours now. That little boy will be home before you know it."

A doctor in scrubs walked out with a chart in his hands and headed toward them. "Mr. or Mrs. Wilson?"

"That's us." Duke's father held up a finger. "How is he?"

"We got the x-rays back. Broken in two places and we're going to have to pin it if we want it to heal properly. Right now he's pretty drugged up but insists on talking to Cora." He glanced at the group. "I can give you five minutes then we want to get him down to theatre."

Cora grabbed Babs hand. "Come with me, please."

The doctor nodded and they both followed him through the door while Duke waited with his brother and father. How the heck was this going to turn out? He turned to Adam. "This wasn't your fault. You know that, right?"

His brother scowled at him. "If you can blame yourself

for my son going missing, don't you think I have the same right here?"

"No." He paused and glanced at his father. "Neither of us are to blame. I get that but what we can do is make sure we get Toby back. One day we'll get Daniel home as well. I firmly believe that, Adam."

His brother looked away but Duke saw the glimmer of tears in his eyes. "Yeah, me too. But that day can't come soon enough."

CHAPTER EIGHTEEN

Babs cooked food that nobody would eat just to keep herself from going crazy but nobody tried to stop her. Cora paced the kitchen back at the ranch, too wound up to sit down. Duke reached out a hand but she kept on pacing.

"It's my fault, Duke. If I hadn't moved this wouldn't have happened."

He dropped his hand. "Honey, that's not true. I think he just decided to do what you said he always does, cause trouble."

She turned to him, desperate for some common sense. "Really? Do you think so?"

"Can you think of any other reason why he'd take Toby? It's not like he's ever expressed any inclination to be a real father, is it?"

She stopped pacing. "No, he hasn't. Not once." Cora blew a long breath out and stared at him. "I wonder what he's after then. Money maybe."

Babs spoke up from the stove where she stirred a pot of chili. "I want to know who told him where you were, sugar."

"Me too. It's not like I tried to hide it but I never announced it to the world either. Just left my change of address with Bo at the restaurant. He wouldn't have told anyone."

Duke held up a finger. "Maybe one of his staff would've without realizing why you left. Is that possible?"

She shrugged. "I guess so."

Jack Snr rushed into the kitchen, his cell phone in his hand. "They found him. Clay is on his way."

"My baby? He's okay?" She tried to push past Jack as Duke grabbed her hand.

"Honey, it's okay. Breathe."

"I need to see him." She started to shake. This was her worst nightmare. The worst afternoon of her life. Cora wouldn't believe he was safe until she saw him.

"They'll be here soon, Cora." Jack smiled through his tears. "Clay called me from his car. They're only minutes away."

"Oh my goodness." Babs threw down her apron and followed them out to the back porch.

A blur of flashing colored lights passed the house and stopped outside the kitchen door followed by the whirr of a police siren. Everyone charged the steps at once.

Cora was the first to reach the car. "Toby?"

The sheriff opened his door and got out. "Little guy wanted a lift home and I promised him lights."

Toby glanced at her from the front seat. "Mom, I got to play the siren and the lights. Clay said I could."

She pulled open the door and scrambled in beside her

son. She patted him down, looking for cuts or bruises, finding none. Her baby was back! She stroked a hand over his face, brushed at the dirty smear on his cheek making sure there was no injury. He grinned at her, tried to shuffle out of her arms. Cora held tight. "You're okay? You're not hurt?"

Toby shrugged. "Nah, I'm alright." He peeked out over her shoulder. "Is Grandpa here?"

Cora took off his seatbelt and pulled him from the car, settled him on her hip, loathe to let him go. Everyone milled around them and peppered Clay with questions. He held his hand up for quiet. "All in good time, folks. Let Cora get Toby something to eat and cleaned up while we discuss this out of the way, okay? He's fine, I double checked him out before I brought him home."

"Sure, Clay." Duke patted his brother on the shoulder. "Let's all go inside, shall we? Mama has a pot of chili on the stove."

Babs grabbed Cora's trembling hand. "Take him upstairs for a shower, sugar. There's a change of clothes in your old room."

"Good idea. I'll help you, okay?" Duke put a hand on Cora's back and guided her inside as everyone milled around Clay peppering him with questions. She didn't care right now.

I almost lost him. She breathed in the little boy smell she never thought she'd get to indulge in again. All she wanted to do was hold her son and thank her lucky stars that she had him back alive.

❧

Duke passed Cora a large towel as she turned off the shower. "Hungry, young man?"

"Yeah, I guess. My belly is sore." He rubbed his tummy and right on time, it grumbled. Toby doubled over in a bout of laughter. "We missed lunch." Cora got him dressed in pj's before he started asking questions. "How's Grandpa? Is he okay?"

"He will be. His leg is broken but the doctors operated and fixed him up. He's gonna have to lay low for a few weeks. Guess you don't know anyone who can take over any of his chores do you?" Duke rubbed his chin, thinking.

Toby's face lit up. "Me, me, me, me. I can do it. I know what he does and I'm good at those things." He paused for breath and turned to Cora. "I can do it, Mom. I can."

She smiled. "I know you can, honey. Why don't we go downstairs for some dinner and you can talk to Adam about it, okay?"

Toby took off as she was trying to do up his buttons and flew down the stairs. They could hear him calling for Adam before he reached the bottom step.

Cora stood and wiped a shaky hand over her brow. She swayed and put a hand out to steady herself but stumbled. Duke reached for her before she broke down. "It's okay, honey I've got you." He held her to his chest as the tears fell. Delayed reaction, he understood that. She'd stayed calm until Toby was out of the room and that took a lot of nerve. He couldn't begin to understand what she must have felt like, how she managed to keep it all together. He was a wreck thinking about all the things that could've happened so she must have been a hot mess and she held it all in.

"You're so strong, Cora. So strong. I can't begin to imagine what must have been going through your head but he's safe now. I'm sure Clay will have John in custody and he won't be going anywhere soon apart from back to jail."

She gave a shuddering laugh. "I don't feel strong. I'm utterly terrified thinking about what he could've done."

Duke reached for a tissue from the bathroom sink and handed it to her. When she cleared away the tears she tried to smile at him but it came off wobbly. "He's safe now and that's all that matters."

"Yeah, he is. Thanks to your brother." Her shoulders slumped and she blew out a breath. "Let's go down and see him I want to thank him properly for finding Toby."

Duke held her hand as they walked downstairs. Laughter came from the dining room where the family had gathered to eat. Everyone was acting as if nothing had happened and he knew it was for Toby's benefit. As they walked in, his mom indicated two seats at the end of the table where places were set for them. "Sit."

Clay looked up from his bowl. "It's really good, guys. Eat up and we'll chat later. I'm off duty now so no hurry, okay?"

Duke got the underlying message. It could all wait until Toby was asleep and out of earshot.

"Thanks. I'm not sure I could eat anything though." Cora grimaced as Babs pushed over a bowl.

"Eat up. You'll feel better once you eat, Cora." She passed another bowl to Duke. "Trust me on this. A full belly helps you cope."

Duke nudged her. "I wouldn't argue if I was you. Not with Mama in a crisis."

Cora smiled and picked up a spoon, taking the first mouthful. "It's good."

Later that evening, once Toby was in bed upstairs with Babs reading him a story, Duke and Cora sat in the lounge with Adam and his father talking to Clay.

The sheriff leaned forward with his elbows on his knees. "He was spotted dragging Toby through a pasture. Appears his car broke down or ran out of gas, or he may have noticed the roadblocks we'd set up. Anyway, the guy that called it in had heard it on the radio and knew right away that it was the guy we were looking for. He called me and we managed to get Toby away from him without too much trouble. That little man of yours is pretty savvy when it comes to taking care of himself."

"What do you mean?" Cora leaned forward, her hands clasped between her knees.

"Safest thing for us to do was send in the dogs. We warned him first but he ignored us. There was always the possibility that Toby could get hurt but our dogs are extremely well trained to go for adults, especially the ones with weapons. Instead of freaking out, Toby hit the dirt face down and lay still while our suspect tried to flee. Clever move. Most kids would've tried to run."

"That's good then." Adam cleared his throat and wiped a hand around the back of his neck. "I, ah, I told him to do that if he ever found himself in a pasture with a beast he didn't know. I didn't want him to run and get mauled. Kinda worried that he'd head into somewhere that wasn't safe for him as he's not really used to living on a ranch." He glanced at Cora then Duke, a self-conscious smile on his face.

"You did good, brother, real good."

Cora stood and went to hug him. "Thank you, Adam. Thank you so much." She turned to Clay. "I can't thank you enough for getting him back safely to me. You have no idea how much I was freaking out."

"Dad told me what he did to Toby when he was little and that was the main reason for calling in the dogs. We were prepared for whatever he tried, that's why we went in the way we did instead of trying to negotiate. I wasn't prepared to risk Toby with someone so unstable. I, ah, I read the police report too so I wasn't expecting this to go as well as it did."

"You did?"

Clay looked a bit embarrassed when Cora gave him a hug too. "Just doing my job, Cora."

"Yeah, well, to me it means a lot. This family has done more for me in the past few weeks than I could ever imagine."

Duke stood and held her against his chest. "And we'd all do it again if you needed us to. You're one of us now, Cora. Don't forget that."

He glanced over her head at his brothers and father. They all stared back with a knowing look in their eyes. Duke had found his family and they approved.

His mom wandered back into the room. "That little man is out for the count. I did tell him you'd carry him home when you were ready, Cora. He wants to sleep in his own bed tonight and he wants that little dog of his."

"We left her with the other dogs down in the barn when we went out today. I'll make sure I send her up to the cottage before I go to sleep." Adam wiped a hand through his hair and smiled at them all. "I'll say goodnight, folks. It's been an eventful day."

"Thank you, Adam. The door isn't locked so if you let her inside, I'd appreciate it." Cora snuggled against Duke with her arm around his back.

Duke lifted a hand in farewell. "Yeah, thanks bro. I'll see you in the morning before I head to the restaurant."

Adam grabbed his hat and kissed his mom on the cheek. "Sure thing. Night y'all."

Duke waited a few moments before he turned to his brother. "Any news on Daniel, Clay?"

Clay shook his head. "Nope. I still have feelers out. If Lissa pops her head up anywhere, I'll know about it."

"I can't believe it's been so long. Where could she have gone?"

"It's a big country, son. She could hide out anywhere for a long time. All we can do is pray that we get him back sooner rather than later." He stretched his arms above his head and got up out of his chair. "I might turn in too. It's been a big day and I promised your mama I'd visit Grandpa early and take him some home cooking."

Duke laughed. "They feed them in hospital, Mama."

She lifted her chin. "You think I don't know that, Duke? But it ain't my home cooking is it? If Grandpa has to stay in for a few days or a week, whatever. We'll make sure he has the good food he's used to. None of that processed food for Grandpa."

"Your food is amazing, Babs. I wouldn't complain if you fed me in hospital, that's for sure." Cora laughed and patted Duke on the arm. "Listen, I'm beat. I want to go home."

He stood up. "Let me carry Toby for you. And I don't

want to see you at work tomorrow. Spend the time home. You've been working too hard anyway."

Babs agreed. "You have, sugar. Take a couple of days with your little man and relax. Duke can cope without you for a day or two. So long as he doesn't go overdoing things, it'll be fine."

"Mama, I'm okay. Stop worrying." He shared a glance with his father. "I've never been this calm before."

She pursed her lips. "Perhaps but I know what you're like, son. Won't take you long to get back to your bad habits if nobody keeps an eye on you."

"Don't worry, Babs. I'll keep him on the straight and narrow. You can count on that." Cora leaned in to kiss her goodnight before reaching for his father and doing the same. "Thank you both so much."

"Oh, I'm relying on you to keep him in line, sugar. You can take that to the bank." Babs winked at her.

Cora blushed. "Let's get you home."

CHAPTER NINETEEN

uke held Toby to his chest, the boys head tucked under his chin and his body slack against him as he walked Cora down to the cottage. She opened the door and Toby's puppy came running to meet them. It jumped up at her legs and whined until she picked her up then proceeded to shower Cora with kisses. "You're such a softie, Lilly. Guess playing with the big dogs wasn't all it's cracked up to be."

"The ranch dogs can get rough but I doubt they'd hurt her. She probably missed this young guy more than anything."

"I don't blame her either. Follow me. I'll turn down Toby's bed." She hurried into his room and pulled down the comforter ,and Duke placed the sleeping child on the sheets. Toby barely moved as Cora pulled the cover up and tucked it under his chin. She put the pup on the bed and it tucked into Toby's side, turning a couple of times to get comfortable before settling down.

"Anyone would be forgiven for thinking today was a

normal day looking at those two." Duke put his arm over her shoulders and gazed down at the sleeping boy.

"Yeah. I wasn't expecting it so soon, Duke." A shiver rolled over her skin and she pushed back the bolt of fear that shot up her spine.

"Come out in the lounge and talk to me." He guided her out the bedroom and they sat together on the couch holding hands.

"I feel so vulnerable. Stupid but I never thought he'd try to steal Toby like that. Nor hurt Grandpa. That makes me so sad, to have brought that on him when he's been so good to Toby."

Duke squeezed her hands, a stern look on his face. "You need to stop those thoughts. It wasn't your fault. We don't know the full story yet, why Grandpa got hurt. Clay's going to take his statement tomorrow. It may be that he was trying to save Toby and got injured in the process or John deliberately hurt him to get Toby. But regardless, none of this is your fault. Your ex is to blame and he will pay for it. You can be assured of that."

"Kidnapping will cost him a few more years inside, I suspect." It would be good to know that he wasn't on the streets again. She didn't want to live her life looking over her shoulder.

"Kidnapping, resisting arrest, assault—the list goes on. Clay will make sure he doesn't get out in a hurry so you have nothing to worry about."

"I appreciate that. I don't know how I would've coped if we were back in El Paso."

"Cora, you need to let it go, stop stressing over what-ifs. They don't help anyone. How about I make you a cup of hot chocolate and you go have an early night? Sleep in tomorrow. Make sure you're relaxed enough to come back to work before you do, okay? I don't care how long it takes. I don't want you coming into the restaurant until you're happy to leave Toby again."

It made sense. She trusted his family implicitly but it would be a while before she was ready to let her little man out of her sight. She couldn't have asked for a better boss. "You're too good to me. You know that, right?" A warm glow started in her belly.

"We're good for each other and I'm not just talking about work."

He stared at her with nothing but love in his eyes and she took a breath. Nobody had ever looked at her like this before.

"I like being around you and Toby. We fit and I think we have something special. You feel the same way, don't you?"

"Yes, I do. I'm worried about having a relationship with the boss though." She gave him a smile and tried not to blush.

"I love you, Cora."

"You do?"

"Yes, I do and I think it's great that you're managing the restaurant. Look how many husbands and wives work together and create a great work environment."

Cora gasped. "You've thought that far ahead?"

Duke laughed. "One thing you'll find out about this family is we don't mess around. We're impulsive. We find something we want, and we go for it and that includes relationships. No point in dragging things out if they feel right."

175

She swallowed. Cora would be lying to herself if she didn't admit that she'd imagined them together. "I guess you're right but I don't want to move too fast. I need to let things roll along smoothly before I take the next step. Let's leave marriage out of it for now, okay?"

"Sure but you've been warned." He gave her a cheerful grin and jumped up, then got serious. "I need to know something before I let it go. Do you think you could love me, Cora?"

Her heart fluttered and she blew out a breath. Tell him now? What did she have to lose? "I think I do. I'm leaning that way, Duke but I want to be sure, okay?"

He pressed a kiss to her forehead. "There's my girl. Practical and careful. I like that about you."

"Thanks." *I think.* The problem was, once the words were out of her mouth, would she be able to stop the avalanche of feelings building in her heart? Cautious by nature, Cora was hesitant to be caught up in the rush of new love. But was it already too late for her?

She had to think about her job and her security if things didn't work out. Duke held everything pertaining to her future in his hands. Never before had she been in this position and as much as she wanted to say those words out loud, it scared her to be so vulnerable.

Regardless, it felt like the gate was already open and she was being pushed through it with little protest.

"Let me get you a drink before I go. I think you've had enough excitement for one day and if I start kissing you, who knows where it will stop?"

❧

D uke needed to keep his distance. He was so in love with Cora he couldn't explain it. But if he kissed her now, there was no saying where it would end up. The last thing he wanted was her submitting to his advances because she was grateful or in a high emotional state. He had more respect for her than that.

He put a mug of milk in the microwave and looked through the containers on the shelf for drinking chocolate. Once he'd stirred it through the warm milk, he glanced over at Cora. She sat serenely on the couch, her head tilted to one side watching him.

"What?"

She shrugged. "I don't know what I was thinking. I was enjoying watching you in the kitchen doing something to care for me. That's very sweet of you, Duke."

"Mama brought us up to care for one another and you're one of us now. I couldn't let you go to bed without something to soothe you. Now, how about I put this on the bedside table and leave you to it? I'll talk to you tomorrow."

"Thank you. You have no idea how much I appreciate it."

He carried the mug into the bedroom and put it down, trying not to imagine himself in this bed with her. One day. When he'd wooed her properly and made her his wife, he'd share this room with her. Until then, he had to be the gentleman he was brought up to be.

Cora saw him to the door. "Can you call me in the morning as soon as you know how Grandpa is?"

"Of course I will. Mama will no doubt be down here to check up on you both anyway and she'll have Dad out at the hospital early to see him."

"I'm sure Toby will want to visit as well. I guess it'll hit him in the morning when he goes down to the barn that Grandpa is missing. They were like bonded soldiers, those two. Hardly ever out of sight of each other."

Duke cupped her chin in his hand and lifted her face to his. "Don't you go worrying over anything, okay? We have everything covered, I promise." He kissed her softly on the lips and broke away.

She kept her face turned up to his. "Duke?"

"Yeah?"

In reply, Cora put a hand behind his head and pulled him down for another kiss, a more sensual kiss that lasted long enough to have him regretting his morals. When she moved back, he found it hard to breathe.

"Goodnight." She moved away and closed the door.

This was going to need to be a speedy courtship because Duke didn't think he could take being so close to her and not having her. He walked back to the big house stopping multiple times to glance back at the cottage wishing he was inside with the woman he loved.

CHAPTER TWENTY

Cora put the last of the breakfast dishes in the drying rack as the sound of a car pulling up the following morning caught her attention.

Clay parked in front of the cottage and got out of his car. Before he could knock on the door, Cora opened it and met him outside. "Clay, is everything alright?"

He nodded and took off his Stetson. "Thought you'd like to hear what happened. He's fronting court later today and will be charged with a handful of offences that will keep him inside until Toby's in his teens. I wanted to let you know that you don't have to worry about him anymore."

She blinked to stop the tears rising. Even though John had been arrested, she still had the irrational fear that he would get out and come for her again. Now she felt she could breathe easier. "Thank you. You have no idea how much better that makes me feel. How's Grandpa? I was just going to go and see Babs and ask her."

Clay leaned on his car and smiled. "I called in early to

talk to him. He's fine and told me to pass on a message to you. 'Don't worry.'" He wiped a hand over his jaw and he had shadows under his eyes as if he hadn't slept.

"What happened? How did he get hurt? Will he be okay?"

"You know they were with Adam getting feed and he was loading the truck? Well, seems Grandpa wanted to show Toby the pens of chickens and turkeys at the back of the feed barn and stopped to check out the butterflies on the way, and your ex came up behind them, kicked Grandpa in the back of the knee and grabbed your son. The old man wouldn't have been much of a threat to him but seemed he only had one thing on his mind and that was taking Toby."

"Did John say why he took him?"

Clay shook his head. "No. Not saying a thing. I got that story from Grandpa who said to tell you he's just fine and you're not to worry. He should be home in about a week but will be laid low for a month or so at least. His leg is pinned and he's going to have issues getting around. Mama will take care of him though. It's what she does best."

"She does. She's been wonderful to us."

"She's pretty good. Easier just to give in and go with the flow. Now, I'd like to talk to Toby. I won't upset him if I can help it but I need to hear what happened from his point of view. Find out if there were any threats made while John had him."

"I understand that. He's down at the barn with Adam. I thought he might sleep in considering but no. He was awake and ready to make up for Grandpa not being here. Said it was his job. I'll walk you down." They both turned down the tree lined driveway and headed to the barn. A soft breeze rustled the leaves, the mooing of the cattle a distant backdrop.

Cora sighed and took a deep breath. "It must have been so nice growing up here with all the freedom to roam these gorgeous pastures. Toby is loving it." She lifted a hand to shield her eyes from the sun. "I can't even imagine being back in the city when I could be here picking these gorgeous Texas blue bonnets."

Clay glanced over at her and smiled. "So, you and Duke, eh? It's good to see my brother happy. He needed someone special. Glad it was you."

"He's a very special man."

"That he is."

They followed the sound of constant chatter and found Toby giving the new calf a bottle, Adam standing outside the fence giving him encouragement. Her baby crouched in the pen on the bed of fresh hay, a huge smile on his face. The earthy smell of cows and fresh manure did nothing to distract her from the sheer pleasure on her babies face. "Mom, look. He's the greediest calf I've ever met." Milk bubbles dribbled from the calf's mouth and landed on Toby's boots before sliding into the hay.

Clay leaned over the rail and shook his head. "I have to agree with you, Toby. He's going to be a great bull one day and you can proudly say you helped raise him."

Toby grinned and took a step backwards when the calf nudged the almost empty bottle. "Wow, stop it." He scrambled over to the side of the pen and Clay easily lifted him up to sit on the top rail. "Thank you. He's a bit pushy, you know." He handed the empty bottle to Cora and she took it passing it off to Adam, and waited for Clay to speak.

"I spoke to Grandpa this morning. He told me to say hi to you and told me how brave you were yesterday."

Toby shrugged and hung his head. "He was a bad man hurting Grandpa like that."

"He was. But I won't let him hurt anyone again, Toby. To do that, I need you to tell me what happened. In your own words and take your time. I'm not in any hurry, now."

Cora placed a hand on her son's back and listened with her heart in her mouth as Toby relayed yesterday's events for Clay.

After he finished giving Clay the details, Toby stared at him intently. "Will he go to jail for hurting Grandpa?"

"Yes, he will."

"Good. He's a bad daddy. I don't want to see him anymore 'cause it's not nice to hurt people. He's not my dad anymore."

Cora shared a glance with Clay. She wasn't sure that Toby would recognize the father who had tried to kill him when he was tiny. "You don't have to, honey. We're going to surround ourselves with people that love and protect us from now on."

Toby looked out over the pasture and sighed. "Can we stay here forever, Mom? I feel safe here."

"I hope so, baby. I certainly hope so."

Clay lifted him off the rail. "I don't think Mama is going to let you guys go anywhere, Toby. And Adam needs you to help him out with the calves. Now, I wanted to go and see my mom and see if she has any cake and coffee going. You two want to join me?"

Toby clapped his hands. "Yes please. She makes great cake."

He scurried out of the barn waving to Adam and Clay and Cora followed. "You have a great little boy there, Cora. I'm so glad we got him back."

Duke pulled back into the driveway in front of the big house. He'd been to see Grandpa and called into the restaurant to make sure everything was under control but he wanted to hold Cora in his arms and tell her all about Grandpa and what happened yesterday.

He slammed his truck door as she came up the drive with Clay and Toby running ahead of them.

"Hey." He waved his hand and met them at the kitchen door. "I've seen Grandpa. Thought you'd like to hear how he is." He pulled Cora into his arms and kissed her forehead.

"Clay told me he's seen him too. What did you think? Is he going to be okay? I feel so guilty for what happened."

Duke shared a glance with his brother. "Didn't you tell her it wasn't her fault?"

"I sure did. Maybe you'll have better luck. I need cake and coffee—so does Toby. We'll leave you two to sort out your issues alone."

Toby giggled. "I can't have coffee. I'm a little kid."

Clay ruffled his hair. "True. You can have cake and milk then." They walked inside and Duke smiled. Trust his brother to know when he needed time alone with Cora. He put his arm around her shoulders and walked her a little way from the house. "Listen, I need to talk to you seriously but don't freak out."

She put a hand to her mouth and her eyes widened.

"It's nothing bad."

The look of concern slowly faded. Cora relaxed. "Okay then, so long as it's a good talk. Not sure I can take anything horrible after yesterday. I want positive vibes only, please."

He put his hands around her waist and took a deep breath. "Right. You know I really, really like you, love you actually. Not sure if I said the words out loud or thought them but I love you more than I can say."

She smiled. "You kind of told me the other night."

His shoulders relaxed a little. "That's good and I'll never stop telling you. But here's the thing. I mentioned that we don't mess around, right? Well, after I saw Grandpa and checked out the restaurant, I knew I had to come straight home and see you." He swallowed down his emotion when a small smile lifted the corners of her lips.

"I know this is fast but I can't help myself. Yesterday was the worst day of my life thinking we were going to lose Toby. I can't imagine what you must have felt because I felt like crap, like my world had just about ended. It made me think, you know. Last night when I left you, all I wanted to do was turn around and grab you. Hold you and not let you go but I don't want a casual affair. I want a forever, Cora. And that forever is with you."

He paused for breath and hoped like heck that she wasn't going to break his heart.

Emotion filled her eyes and her lips parted. "You want to take us on forever with the baggage we have?"

"It's not baggage, it's a past and we all have one. I want a future with you and if that means we have to deal with your ex as part of it, so be it. We can do it together as a family."

"Are you sure, Duke?"

"I've never been more sure of anything in my life." He dropped one arm and struggled to get the small box from his back pocket and opened it.

Cora stared at the solitaire diamond he held up for her to see.

"Cora, will you marry me?"

She blinked a couple of times before she spoke. "Yes. I'll marry you, Duke."

He picked her up and swung her around, his heart bursting with joy. It wasn't until he put her down and slid the ring on her finger that he heard the noises coming from the house. Mama came hurrying down to meet them, her arms wide and tears streaking down her cheeks.

"You beautiful people. So very happy for you both." She flung her arms around each of them, smothering them in kisses.

"Mama, it's not nice to listen to other people's conversations." Duke tried to chastise her but knew he was wasting his time. Mama was Mama and that wasn't going to change any time soon.

"What do you expect? A little bird told me you bought the ring and I could barely contain myself. Come in and have cake to celebrate. We have a wedding to plan."

Duke smiled and grabbed Cora's hand pulling her toward the house. "See what happens when the jeweller is a family friend? Nobody can keep a secret in Wishbone. Welcome to my big, wacky family."

THANK YOU

Thank you for reading Texas Cowboy, Book One of the Wishbone Texas Series. You're a rockstar! I hope you enjoyed reading it as much as I loved writing it.

As you know, reviews are the lifeblood of our work. They not only help future readers find new authors to read, but also help me gain spots of various advertising platforms.

I would be grateful if you could do me a favour and leave a review at your favourite outlet.

ABOUT THE AUTHOR

Bestselling Author, Ann B Harrison takes you to the places she loves the best. The wide open countryside of Montana where cowboys roam free and the ever changing Australian Outback where no two days are the same.

Ann lives in the beautiful Hunter Valley with her own handsome hero of many years. She has always loved the ups and downs of life in small communities and she shares this with readers in her novels.

Strong sexy heroines with a good dash of sass thrown in feature in her stories. Of course these women need an equally strong man to complete the story. Bring on the hero and watch the passion ignite.

When not writing Ann enjoys reading, gardening, and walking her very cute dogs Molly and Chilli.

Want to sign up for her mailing list and keep up to date? You can sign up at www.annbharrisonauthor.com

facebook.com/Ann-B-Harrison-Author-311207972338638
instagram.com/ann_b_harrison_author
bookbub.com/authors/ann-b-harrison

Mitch

Audrey

Wishbone Texas

(Contemporary Western Romance)

Texas Cowboy

Texas Lawman

Texas Crooner

Texas Healer

Hope Harbor

(Contemporary Women's Fiction)

Forever This Time

Hold Me Now

Don't Let Go

Worth Fighting For

Foxborough Hall

(Historical Mystery Thriller)

Billionaires Club

(Contemporary Romance)

Second Chance Billionaire

Curse of Kin

(Young Adult Paranormal)

Witchling

Changling

Treason

Ingram Content Group UK Ltd.
Milton Keynes UK
UKHW040800240723
425668UK00001B/18